# ONLY THE VALET WILL DO

## SOPHIE BARNES

ALSO BY SOPHIE BARNES

*Novels*

**Brazen Beauties**

Mr. West and The Widow

Mr. Grier and The Governess

Mr. Dale and The Divorcée

**Diamonds in the Rough**

The Dishonored Viscount

Her Scottish Scoundrel

The Formidable Earl

The Forgotten Duke

The Infamous Duchess

The Illegitimate Duke

The Duke of Her Desire

A Most Unlikely Duke

**The Crawfords**

Her Seafaring Scoundrel

More Than a Rogue

No Ordinary Duke

**Secrets at Thorncliff Manor**

Christmas at Thorncliff Manor

His Scandalous Kiss

The Earl's Complete Surrender

Lady Sarah's Sinful Desires

**At The Kingsborough Ball**

The Danger in Tempting an Earl

The Scandal in Kissing an Heir

The Trouble with Being a Duke

**The Summersbys**

The Secret Life of Lady Lucinda

There's Something About Lady Mary

Lady Alexandra's Excellent Adventure

**Standalone Titles**

The Girl Who Stepped Into The Past

How Miss Rutherford Got Her Groove Back

*Novellas*

**Diamonds in the Rough**

The Roguish Baron

**The Enterprising Scoundrels**

Mr. Clarke's Deepest Desire

Mr. Donahue's Total Surrender

**The Townsbridges**

An Unexpected Temptation

A Duke for Miss Townsbridge

Falling for Mr. Townsbridge

Lady Abigail's Perfect Match

When Love Leads To Scandal

Once Upon a Townsbridge Story

**The Honorable Scoundrels**

The Duke Who Came To Town

The Earl Who Loved Her

The Governess Who Captured His Heart

**Standalone Titles**

Sealed with a Yuletide Kiss (An historical romance advent calendar)

The Secrets of Colchester Hall

Mistletoe Magic (from Five Golden Rings: A Christmas Collection)

Miss Compton's Christmas Romance

# CHAPTER ONE

Lady Lilliana Enshaw, known to her friends as Lilli, gazed at the translucent piece of quartz in the palm of her hand. The delicate chain attached to one end slid over her fingers like liquid gold.

"Thank you, Eva." Excitement coursed through Lilli's veins as she spoke to her cousin, the Countess of Somerset. "You cannot imagine how long I've looked forward to wearing this."

"You've had to wait the longest, which can't have been easy." Eva offered a soft smile and sipped her tea. "But with three successful weddings as proof of the stone's matchmaking powers, I'm sure you'll meet your future husband soon."

Lilli prayed Eva was right, for she yearned to fall headlong into her own romantic adventure. As happy as she was for her cousins, Eva, Annie, and Henrietta, who'd all gotten married within the past year, it was difficult not to be envious of the loving glances and sweet endearments they frequently shared with their husbands.

"I hope so." She carefully fastened the chain around her neck so the stone hung snugly against her skin, immediately above the décolletage of her lilac gown. "Unfortunately, my parents and I will be leaving London for Stratham House next week. I don't anticipate forming any attachment while I'm there since no one else will be joining us besides Henry. So I fear I may have to wait until next year's Season to find my true love."

One would think that by being the daughter of the Earl and Countess of Stratham and the sister of Viscount Islington, one would have every chance in the world of meeting one's intended. Not in Lilli's experience.

"I doubt that will be the case," Eva said. "Don't fret, Lilli. I'm sure the stone will surprise you as much as it did me. Perhaps with a duke who's passing by or maybe a friend of Henry's."

Lilli appreciated Eva's encouragement though she failed to see how one of the last unmarried dukes in England would suddenly come knocking when none of them had familiar ties with her family. As for her brother, Henry's, friends, she'd met them all and hadn't been impressed.

Besides, Henry had specifically informed Mama that he would be coming alone. Which meant there would be no one to make Lilli's heart beat faster for some time yet.

She expelled a breath and accepted this truth. As

eager as she was to get on with a courtship, she didn't feel the same sort of urgency as had her eldest cousin, Annie, who'd almost been on the shelf by the time the rose quartz crystal – and what it could do – had been discovered in their grandmother's attic.

With regard to marriage, Lilli had time. She was only nineteen, so things weren't too dire yet, but that didn't make her less impatient. She'd always been the sort of person who craved activity and action. She disliked having to sit still and wait for any reason. Worst of all, she hated feeling as though she lacked control – the ability to get things done through her own force of will.

"Thank you for stopping by," she said when Eva prepared to leave, "and for giving me the pendant."

"You mustn't fret," Eva said, taking Lilli's hand and giving it a gentle squeeze. "The stone will see you happy before you know it."

Rather than voice her concerns, Lilli nodded and saw her cousin out. She then climbed the stairs to her bedchamber where she began compiling a list of all the things she would have to take with her to Stratham House next week. Between her science journals, the edition of *Much Ado about Nothing* she planned on re-reading, a few new adventure novels, her diary and correspondence, she hoped to distract herself from the cravings of her heart.

~

Seated in the well-sprung carriage belonging to his employer, Viscount Islington, Tristan Henley reviewed the tasks he'd jotted down for himself in a slim, leather-bound, pocket notebook. Number one, purchase a new bottle of sandalwood oil to replace the nearly depleted one he'd packed for Islington.

Next, he had to remember to write another response to the Earl of Fretmire on Islington's behalf, turning down the invitation to visit him. Islington had answered the first letters himself, politely declining. But when the earl had grown more persistent, Tristan had promised to step in and handle the situation since Fretmire, who wanted a match between his daughter and Islington, refused to take a hint.

Tristan considered how to best phrase the letter, then paused to reflect. Perhaps, before seeing to tasks one and two, he ought to inform the cook at Stratham House of Islington's newfound fondness for crêpes, which he preferred for breakfast instead of eggs, bacon, and toast.

"You're very quiet today." Islington spoke from the opposite bench, his voice pensive. "I hope there's nothing troubling you."

"Not at all," Tristan said. "I'm only making some mental notes."

He closed his notebook and gave his employer his full attention. He wasn't so much troubled as wary and determined. Because he needed this job and the impressive salary it provided.

Many men in his position would think it beneath

them to work, but beggars couldn't be choosers and Tristan sorely needed the money. And since he'd grown accustomed to handling his own clothes and shoes as the family budget tightened and servants departed, he'd been prepared for the unusual position Islington had sought to fill. His only regret was the lie he'd told in order to secure the job. But if Islington had any inkling of who his valet truly was, Tristan feared he'd have turned him away.

Instead, he'd enjoyed three months of employment with a man he might have called a friend had his own situation been different. But fate had dealt a rough hand from which Tristan could see no immediate escape. Not that he minded. Serving the viscount had provided him with a new purpose along with the means by which to enjoy a visit to Cornwall.

"You work too hard," Islington said, his firm voice scattering Tristan's thoughts once more.

"I'd have thought that a welcome trait in an employee," Tristan said.

Islington tilted his head. "For some, perhaps, but I am not the sort of man who enjoys working others to the point of exhaustion. And besides, you're my valet, which literally makes you my closest confidante. I'd not mind having a leisurely chat with you on occasion. Least of all when we're stuck together for several hours without other form of distraction."

Tristan answered Islington's warm expression with a smile. "My apologies. Is there a particular subject you'd like to discuss?"

"Let's start with my sister."

Tristan almost choked on his own tongue. "Pardon?"

Schooling his features, Islington locked gazes with Tristan. "Lady Lilliana is as spirited as they come, and while I adore this about her, it's a characteristic destined to land her in trouble. In London, friends and family have always been kind enough to help keep her out of it. In Cornwall, however, she has more freedom. While there's little for her to get up to in the ways of causing a scandal, I fear for her safety."

"How so?" Tristan asked, his posture rigid and his mind in sudden turmoil. Babysitting what sounded to him like a willful hoyden had not been part of the job description.

"For starters, she has a history of getting wet, damaging her clothes, climbing into high places, sneaking off to secret hideouts and..." Islington grinned. "Don't take me wrong. She's a gently bred lady, but there is an adventurous streak to her that could use some taming."

"Sounds like she needs to get married," Tristan remarked before he could think better of it. He blinked. "My apologies. I did not mean to suggest–"

"That's quite all right. Papa and I have already discussed it. In fact, part of the reason I'm going to Stratham House instead of to Bath as initially planned is so I can help talk some sense into her. And since you've been introduced to most of my social circle by now, I'm hoping you'll advise me on the most suitable prospects. After all, Lilli is my sister, so I want her to be happy."

Tristan wasn't sure how he managed to smile at the idea of playing matchmaker to a young woman he'd never met – an earl's daughter, no less. Teeth gritted behind stretched lips, he wondered if he'd been too hasty in appreciating his position. Clearly there was more to it than he could ever have dreamed possible. And rather than look forward to reaching Stratham House as he'd done when they'd set off that morning, he now dreaded it with every fiber of his being.

# CHAPTER TWO

Upon her arrival at Stratham House, Lilli leapt from the family carriage before the footman had a chance to put down the steps. Behind her, Mama and Papa cautioned her to be careful, but Lilli turned a deaf ear. After sitting for several hours, she was eager to stretch her legs.

"When did you get here?" she asked her brother, who must have been waiting for their arrival since he was already descending the front steps. He strode toward her with a grin, his arms wide and ready for the embrace she always gave him when they met.

"Two days ago." He hugged her against him, holding her tight for a moment before he greeted their parents. "How was your journey?"

"Trouble free," Papa said. "Provided you discount your sister's constant pestering. I swear, it doesn't matter how old she gets. She still can't be still or silent for more than five minutes."

This was not said in a critical tone but with

warmth. It prompted Mama to chuckle while she smoothed her skirts. Lilli's cheeks warmed with the pleasure of knowing that while she might be more boisterous than most young ladies her age, her family loved her no matter what.

She eyed Henry with interest. He looked…different. "Is that a new jacket?"

Henry's lips twitched. "It is indeed."

"And am I mistaken or is that the most exquisite cravat knot you've ever seen?" Papa asked Mama while eyeing Henry's throat.

"It's certainly more elaborate than any I've seen Henry wear before." Mama peered at him, her gaze shifting over his perfectly pressed breeches until it settled upon his glossy boots. Her eyebrows lifted as she looked back up. "Your style has always been rather relaxed. Now, there's a certain dashingness about you."

"Dashingness?" Lilli queried. "Is that a word?"

"If you must know," Henry said before Mama could respond, "I've acquired a new valet who also carries out the occasional secretarial duties. A bit unusual, I'll admit, but you know how I hate having too many servants around me. This way, most of my daily needs are met by one man. He's a very meticulous fellow. Goes by the name of Mr. Henley. I'll introduce you to him shortly."

"Well," Papa said. "I'll have to thank him when you do, for I daresay your mother is right. Judging from this new appearance of yours, I've no doubt you'll get yourself married in no time at all."

Lilli couldn't help but laugh at her brother's horrified expression.

"You *are* the eldest," she murmured to him as they started up the front steps. "It's only fair you should find yourself wed before I."

"Not if I can help it," he whispered back.

As much as she loved pretending indignation, she hoped her brother was right. Beneath her spencer she felt the cool press of the rose quartz crystal she'd worn for nearly a week. It hadn't led to an unexpected encounter with her future husband yet. The question now was whether or not it would and how long it might take.

No sense in worrying over something she could not control, Lilli decided. She'd simply have to be patient and wait. After having refreshments in the parlor, Lilli changed out of her traveling clothes and set off for a brisk walk. She'd spent her childhood at Stratham House. She loved the property with its wild gardens where roses climbed stone walls and lavender still filled the air with sweet fragrance. It welcomed her with its familiarity and beckoned for her to explore.

Enjoying the crunch of gravel beneath her feet, she strode past the pond to where the woods began. She'd built hideouts in there with Henry many years ago, had climbed a particular oak from which she'd felt as though she could view the entire kingdom, and had chased after squirrels and rabbits until her clothes had been well and truly ruined.

A grin pulled at her lips on that thought. While London might be more conducive to finding her soul mate, it could be horribly stifling. At least here in the countryside she was free to be herself. Within reason, she amended as she headed along a well–travelled path the game keeper used when he rode out to set traps and hunt.

The weather was pleasantly cool without being chilly. Soon the leaves would begin turning various shades of orange, yellow, and red, but for now they retained their lush green color. Flitting from branch to branch, birds chattered to one another while the faint gurgle of water from a nearby brook added a soothing rhythm.

Upon reaching the tell–tale roots of an uprooted elm, Lilli veered to the right, heading between the foliage of smaller saplings and bushes until she spied her favorite oak. It stood in a clearing, its branches reaching sideways as if attempting to touch other trees.

With the satisfaction born from the deep anticipation of a long desired climb, Lilli quickened her pace. She couldn't wait to survey the surrounding landscape from ten feet above the ground.

Whistling a merry tune she marched ahead and had almost arrived at her destination when the ground disappeared beneath her right foot.

A gasp burst from between her lips. It transformed into a startled yelp as her leg sank farther into the hole, causing her left knee to scrape the ground. Her hands shot out, attempting to break the fall, but the force of her palms connecting with solid ground jolted her bones and twisted her into an awkward position.

Lilli sucked in a breath and gritted her teeth. "Damn and blast."

Palms flat on the ground, she leaned forward, hefted her weight onto the left side of her body, and tried to pull her leg free.

Her foot didn't budge.

"Bloody hell." She scowled at the ground. Where on earth had this hole come from? It hadn't been here on her previous visit. Panting, she made another series of attempts to free herself only to realize that it was no use.

She was stuck and would now have to wait for someone to realize she hadn't returned to Stratham House. No doubt her parents would be the ones to come find her.

Lilli sighed in exasperation.

*Brilliant!*

Tristan knew Islington's family had arrived a couple of hours ago, but since he'd been in no rush to make their acquaintance – or more specifically to make Lady Lilliana's – he'd found a series of tasks to engage in. Like brushing Islington's hats and wiping them clean on the inside so they would look perfect should Islington choose to go out.

After reviewing the dressing room for a third time to ensure all was neat and in order with every item of clothing perfectly folded and wrapped in linen to protect it from dust, Tristan decided it might be prudent to check on the trap he'd prepared that morning.

In his opinion, digging a hole, covering it with foliage, and leaving apple and carrot pieces as bait was the simplest way to catch a rabbit. In London one rarely found a decent sized animal, so he was glad to be away in the countryside where he could put his trap–setting skills to good use.

He took the servants' stairs to the kitchen, grabbed a burlap sack, and headed toward the woods. Islington had told Tristan he needn't trouble himself, that the game keeper would catch whatever was to be served for dinner. But Tristan enjoyed the pursuit and was more than happy to accomplish it when time allowed. So he'd gone out to dig a sizeable hole three hours before his master usually arose and expected Tristan to help him with his toilette.

Branches reached across to the path leading into the woods, obscuring the sky. A woodpecker hammered its beak against a tree while what sounded like a goldfinch twittered among the canopies.

Tristan strode forward, his boots disturbing some of last year's left over leaves which had since turned muddy. With the burlap sack slung over one shoulder, he reached a fallen elm, then turned off the path. A shrew scampered away, disappearing into the under-growth at the exact same time Tristan heard a series of expletives coming from nearby.

"I'll murder whoever did this," came the next words, followed by additional curses.

Tristan quickened his pace. It sounded like

someone required assistance and judging from the tone, that someone was a woman. But what he didn't expect was for said woman to be the quarry he'd caught in his trap.

Blistering barnacles.

He ran forward and fell to the ground beside her. "Allow me to help."

Hazel eyes, more green than brown, met his and for a brief moment his world stood still. The only movement Tristan registered was the rapid beat of his heart. Never in his life had he–

"I believe you offered assistance?"

He blinked and quickly shook himself free from the snare he'd been caught in. "My apologies."

Humor tugged at the edge of the woman's pink lips, slanting her mouth while a blush tinged her cheeks. When she spoke next, her voice was softer, perhaps even a little bit timid. "I'm just glad you happened along when you did. The position I'm in is not particularly comfortable, so if you don't mind, I'd like to get up. Provided you're able to free me."

Noting that her leg was knee deep in the hole, Tristan hesitated. He swallowed. "If you'll permit, I'd like to reach inside the hole, along the length of your leg, in order to find the obstruction."

When she didn't reply he glanced at her face again and saw that her color had deepened. She stared at him as if he'd asked for her hand in marriage. But then she slowly nodded, as if with a great deal of thought behind the gesture.

Tristan's pulse quickened. His stomach tightened. It

was the most peculiar thing, but it occurred to him that he'd been holding his breath while desperately hoping for her compliance. Because, Lord help him, he'd never longed to touch a woman as much as he longed to touch her. Hell, he had the most inexplicable need to run his fingers through her blonde hair, to trace the edge of her jaw, and to inhale her fragrance.

It made no logical sense. She was a stranger and he ought not be having such inappropriate thoughts. And yet, the moment his hand found the length of her calf and the delicate curve of her ankle, it was as if his every desire came crashing over his head.

Feeling much like an inexperienced youth who'd never encountered a female before, Tristan forced himself to ignore his body's response and to carefully figure out why she was stuck. It didn't take long to discover the tree root looped around her ankle. As impossible as it seemed, her foot had gone straight through it. In her current position, she could not pull her foot out or reach inside the hole to free it with her own hands.

With the utmost care, Tristan wedged his fingers between the root and the woman's ankle, increasing the space. When this didn't help, he grabbed his knife. "I promise you won't be harmed, but I'm going to have to cut you free."

Instead of looking afraid or even the slightest bit hesitant, she gave a swift nod of agreement. "All right."

It occurred to Tristan that finding a woman who remained calm in a situation most would have found untenable was rare. Especially when a stranger suggested wielding a sharp blade close to her flesh. He made the cut before she could change her mind and helped pull her leg out of the hole.

A slim leg, clad in a torn stocking, emerged. It was followed by a soiled leather boot.

Tristan stared as she proceeded to rotate her ankle.

Her slight wince snapped him out of his daze. He shook his head. "Are you all right?"

"I believe so. It hurts only a little." She gave him a timid smile. "Thank you, sir. Your help is much appreciated."

Relieved, Tristan stood and offered his hand to help her rise. The moment she took it, a shock of awareness rushed up his arm. He drew a sharp breath to steady himself only to realize that she looked as dazed as he felt. Was it possible she'd experienced the same inexplicable pull as he?

He studied her appearance. Dressed in a practical gown now marred by dirt and a ripped seam, she must be a maid whose acquaintance he'd not yet made.

Unsure of how to proceed when he didn't know her identity, Tristan released her and quickly confessed, "It was the least I could do since you'd not have been stuck had it not been for me."

She tilted her head, her eyes curious. "Oh?"

"I dug that hole in the hope of catching a rabbit. In other words, I am the man you just expressed a desire to murder."

Lilli's pulse was racing so fast she could scarcely catch her breath. A short while ago she'd been ready to give the person behind the hole a thorough tongue lashing. Now, all she wanted to do was drown in the most gorgeous eyes she'd ever encountered. The warm and welcoming coffee shade made her toes curl in her half boots while the velvety huskiness of her rescuer's voice caused her skin to tingle.

He was handsome beyond compare, his features the sort made for every manner of romantic musings. Sooty lashes blinked at her with sensual slowness while full lips parted with both concern and wonder. Heavy brown locks fell over his forehead, tempting her to reach up and push them aside.

She resisted but…

Lord help her, the moment she'd caught her first proper glimpse of this man, it was as though she'd been reborn. Gone was the stagnant state she'd resigned herself to in recent years. Instead, her body had come alive with the sweetest sense of awareness she'd ever known. It was a craving unlike any other, for him to be near her, to touch her and ease the yearning deep in her heart.

It was without doubt the most wonderfully inappropriate feeling she'd ever encountered. Yet it was over much too soon when he pulled her upright and let her go. She swayed, a little unsteady on her feet though not because she was hurt but rather because he'd managed to weaken her knees.

*Good heavens.*

If she wasn't mistaken, the stone was already

working its magic, for it had clearly brought her a man toward whom she responded with interest instead of indifference. Apparently, her brother had brought a friend with him after all. Of course, she'd yet to make this friend's acquaintance, and although it wasn't proper for them to introduce themselves to each other, Lilli decided she'd had enough of social etiquette. But first, she ought to respond to his comment.

"As I'm sure you can imagine, I was rather put out when I said that." She shrugged one shoulder. "Complaining made me feel better."

"I suppose that explains the cursing."

Heat flooded Lilli's cheeks. "I don't suppose you can forget what you heard?"

He laughed, the sound so deep and full-bodied it instantly filled her with warmth. "Not very likely, I'm afraid. But you need not worry. Truth is, I found it both charming and educational."

Lilli's brow creased with skepticism. "Really?"

"I've heard men say one should go to the devil, but never that one should–"

"Please don't remind me," she groaned, both mortified and oddly at ease at the same time. "I'd hate for you to think ill of my parents for failing with regard to my upbringing."

"I'm sure that would be impossible," he said, the sincerity in his voice diving deep beneath her skin until she feared she might actually sigh with pleasure.

*Idiot.*

"I appreciate your saying so," she told him. When he added nothing further, she decided to say, "I realize we ought to be formally introduced by a mutual acquaintance, but since there is no one else here to see to such matters, perhaps we could make an exception?"

He gave her a quizzical look. "Considering our positions, I see no reason for us to adhere to such protocol."

It was Lilli's turn to be baffled. "Our positions? Surely it is that very thing which denies us the chance to exchange names without supervision. Why, being alone here together is scandalous enough I should think."

His eyes sharpened and then they narrowed. He studied her with an increased degree of intensity. "Who are you, exactly?"

Lilli drew back on account of the sudden firmness in his voice. She produced a nervous laugh. "Lady Lilliana, of course. Who else would I be?"

Her new companion stared at her for a long moment before eventually closing his eyes on a sigh. "Of course." He shook his head and muttered something beneath his breath before executing an elegant bow. "Mr. Tristan Henley, at your service."

Lilli gasped. "You're–"

"Viscount Islington's valet, my lady."

*No.*

*No, no, no.*

This could not be happening. Lilli stared at Mr. Henley in horrified silence. The attraction she felt toward him could not be denied, which had to mean he was the man the stone had brought her. But the idea of an earl's daughter being courted by and eventually marrying a servant was ludicrous in the extreme. Which had to mean the stone had gotten it wrong because this… This was like a cruel joke or some sort of nightmare from which she prayed she would soon awaken.

"I ought to return to the house." Her voice sounded hollow to her own ears. It matched the crippling disappointment now weighing her down.

"Allow me to escort you."

"Thank you, but that will not be necessary." Right now, she wanted to run from him as fast as she could, pretend they'd never met. "Besides, you still have a rabbit to catch."

"The trap will see to that."

"Nevertheless."

He held her gaze for a moment. "What about your ankle?"

"It's fine. I can walk unaided." When he gave a swift nod she dipped her head and turned, walking away and leaving him there without a backward glance even though it felt like her heart was breaking.

# CHAPTER THREE

When Lilli woke the next morning she did so with the certainty of having been wrong about her response to Mr. Henley. Obviously, him being the first young man she'd encountered since acquiring the rose quartz crystal had convinced her of feelings that simply weren't there. How could they be when a match with him would be as impossible as flying to the moon?

With this in mind she rose from bed with renewed determination. While being in the country might limit her social options, it didn't exclude them entirely. Perhaps if she could convince Mama and Papa to invite some local gentry to dinner she might meet someone else, someone to take her interest away from Mr. Henley. Who somehow managed to remain lodged in her brain. As irritating as it was, he'd even invaded her dreams where the soft caress of his fingers against her cheek had…

"Bother." Lilli fixed her attention on the pull of the

comb her lady's maid, Vera, was currently applying to her hair. Locks rolled up with strips of cotton during the night were untied and pinned until Lilli's face was framed by bouncy curls.

"Are you all right, my lady?" Vera asked, pausing in her task. "Did I nick you?"

"No. You're as gentle as always." When she offered no further explanation, Vera finished styling her hair and then dabbed Lilli's favorite jasmine oil to each side of her neck.

Next, she helped Lilli dress after which Lilli made her way down to breakfast. As she approached the dining room, she heard voices coming from what had once been a small sitting room but now served as her brother's study when he was in residence. The door stood slightly ajar, permitting her to hear every perfect word uttered by Mr. Henley.

Lilli shook her head even as liquid heat pooled in her stomach. This was madness. The man was merely listing numbers, no doubt while reviewing the ledgers, yet somehow, against all odds, his voice managed to send the most delicious shivers down her spine.

Annoyed and frustrated by the realization that the hours she'd spent apart from him since their first encounter had not dimmed her foolish desire to be near him, she set her jaw and continued toward the dining room. Thankfully, Mama was still there reading the scandal column she enjoyed every morning once Papa was done with the paper.

After wishing her a good morning, Lilli collected a

plate from the sideboard, filled it with eggs, bacon, and toast, and took her seat at the table.

Mama glanced at her. "How are you feeling today?"

"Perfectly well." Lilli had told her parents she'd tripped and fallen in the woods when they'd questioned her disheveled appearance upon her return yesterday afternoon. "In fact, I'd like to suggest a dinner party."

Mama blinked. "A dinner party?"

"Yes. There are several good families in the area with whom we rarely socialize."

"That is because we do all our socializing in London. When we're here I like to relax without any fuss. Which is why I'm relieved your brother refrained from bringing friends with him this time."

The mention of Henry and his friends reminded Lilli of Mr. Henley. She steeled herself against the hope of spending more time in his company. That would not happen.

"My Seasons have not resulted in an engagement," Lilli pressed, "so maybe it's time to consider a different tactic. If you prefer, we could host a picnic instead since that would be more casual in nature."

Mama dropped the paper and settled her gaze more firmly on Lilli. "I've never known you to be so keen on securing a match before. Indeed, I believe your Seasons proved fruitless due to your own lack of effort. Rest assured, your papa and I have decided it's time for you to set your mind to finding a husband soon, lest you end up on the shelf. But we had thought to wait until spring."

"Doing so won't change my options, which is where the issue lies." Lilli sipped her tea before daring to ask, "Aren't there any young men here in Cornwall who'd make me a suitable match?"

Mama gave a short laugh. "Cornwall is large so I'm sure there are."

"I mean someone I've not yet encountered in London."

"Hmm… It's possible." Mama pursed her lips, the cogs in her brain clearly turning. "I'll set my mind to it later today if you like. After I've finished reading about the scandal involving Lady Gwendolyn."

"The Marquess of Wentworth's daughter?" When Mama nodded, Lilli asked, "What scandal?"

Mama sighed. "The foolish chit was discovered with one of her parents' footmen if you can believe it. Not with a titled rake whom she might have married but with a servant of all people. Now she's been shipped off to Lord knows where, but there's no question she has been permanently ruined and her family's name dragged through the mud. Honestly, I cannot imagine what she was thinking."

With no idea how to respond, Lilli took a bite of succulent bacon and started to chew. The sooner she got her brain occupied with someone other than Mr. Henley, the better. In any event she would strive to avoid him at all cost during the rest of her stay at Stratham House.

～

"Would you care to tell me what's going on?" Islington asked. He regarded Tristan with a probing gaze.

Tristan glanced up from the ledger he was reviewing for the tenth time that morning. The numbers had tallied perfectly the first time he'd gone over them, but when he'd heard Lady Lilliana's voice coming from the hallway half an hour earlier, he'd decided against leaving the study for the time being. It was the best way, he'd reasoned, to avoid her altogether and save himself the sweet torment of being near a woman he had no business feeling the slightest degree of attraction toward.

Deliberately, he gave his employer a blank look. "Forgive me, my lord, but to what do you refer?"

Islington's eyebrows drew together, creating a series of creases upon his brow. "Not even in London do you remain indoors all day. You enjoy a change of pace, I've noted – getting away from my bachelor lodgings for a while to stretch your legs by running errands or performing other tasks. Devil take it, you even partner with me when I practice my fencing or when I desire a game of chess. But since arriving here last week, it's been nearly impossible for me to drag you from this room. Hell, you're always busy with something, whether it be a collar that suddenly needs pressing or an urgent bill you've somehow managed to produce."

*Ah.*

Tristan hadn't realized the viscount was so observant. He'd not said a word until now.

"My apologies, but I believed it prudent to make

myself scarce while here so you can enjoy your family's company without a servant's interference."

This turned Islington's frown into a scowl. "I was of the impression that you and I were more than employer and employee, that we were becoming friends."

"We were, but—"

"I genuinely like you, Mr. Henley, and I enjoy your company. I hope you weren't merely keeping mine on account of duty or because I'm paying your salary."

Realizing his mistake, Tristan gave his head a quick shake. It hadn't occurred to him the viscount might think he was the one Tristan strove to avoid, so he swiftly told him, "I enjoy your company too and value the friendship you've offered thus far."

"Excellent." Islington's grave expression faded. He smiled with such delight the hair at the nape of Tristan's neck stood on end. And then he said, "In that case I would like for you to accompany my sister and me on a ride. It will do you good to get some fresh air and exercise."

God help him.

"My lord, I..." When Islington raised an eyebrow in challenge, Tristan emitted a weary sigh. "Of course. When should I be ready?"

"Is fifteen minutes enough?"

The fact he would even ask was an indication of Islington's respect. Tristan would not risk losing that, not even to guard his own heart. So he nodded and voiced a succinct, "yes."

But when he arrived at the stables and spotted Lady

Lilliana, he knew the day would pose a far greater challenge than he'd expected. Because there she was, dressed in a snug pair of fawn–colored breeches paired with a brown velvet jacket. Tristan scarcely knew where to look without either appearing rude or worse, like a man on the cusp of being devoured by lust.

*Merciful heavens.*

He swallowed past the tightness in this throat and forced his attention to Islington, who stood nearby holding the reins of a gleaming black stallion. How the hell could the man permit his sister to venture outside her bedchamber in such attire? How could he allow Tristan and...and...the stable hands a view of her perfectly formed bottom?

It boggled his mind and ate at his nerves until irritation flooded his veins, mingling with his desire to haul the woman against him and run his hands over those tempting curves. Gritting his teeth, he managed a greeting, which sounded too harsh to his own ears.

Thankfully, no one else seemed to notice the turbulent state of his mind and body. Lady Lilliana for one refused to look in his direction, simply tossing a greeting at him while checking the harness on her horse. Meanwhile, Islington waved Tristan toward a caramel–colored mare named Toffee and told him to lead it outside.

Eager for a task to distract him from the woman he had as much chance of ignoring as he might a blistering headache, Tristan followed Islington out of the stables while focusing every ounce of awareness on the steady clip–clop of hooves against stone. Which worked rather well for a few blissful moments. Until Lady Lilliana strode from the stable as well, swung herself into the saddle with elegant fluidity, and kicked her horse into a trot.

Holy hell.

Tristan shot the viscount a desperate glance, but he was already following his sister, leaving Tristan to pick up the rear and – worst of all – to watch the lady rise and fall against her saddle in ways that threatened to make this the most uncomfortable ride of his life.

There was nothing better than a good ride to rid oneself of agitation, which was why Lilli had chosen to take Nora out for a large part of the day. But when Henry had learned of her excursion, he'd insisted on coming along. Worse yet, he'd decided to ask Mr. Henley to join them – a clear reminder of how very different her brother was from most of his peers. Instead of leaving his valet at home where he belonged, he'd decided to bring him along as he would a friend.

"It isn't healthy for any man to be closeted away all day," Henry had told her when she'd questioned Mr. Henley's joining them. "Besides, I genuinely like him and would rather have his company than one of Mama and Papa's stuffy footmen."

Fearful her brother would grow suspicious if she continued arguing the issue, she'd let the subject slide.

Digging her heels into Nora's flanks, Lilli urged her into a canter and then to a gallop. Knowing Mr. Henley was either in Henry's bedchamber or in the study most days – that she'd find him there if she opened one of those doors – had wreaked havoc on both her body and mind. The fact that he seemed intent on avoiding her had been both gratifying and unnerving in the worst way imaginable.

On one hand, she wanted to explore the pull she'd experienced when they'd first met but on the other, she knew damn well that doing so could prove detrimental, not only to her heart but to her reputation. Now, as she rode, she could feel his gaze searing her until heat shot through her veins.

Excitement thrummed in every fiber of her being – a madness destined to make her act without thinking. Beneath the tight fit of her jacket and the soft linen shirt she'd elected to wear the cool press of quartz tingled against her skin. During the past week she'd pondered the path it had laid out before her. The picnic she'd suggested would happen tomorrow, which would hopefully help her meet a more suitable prospect than her brother's employee.

Honestly, the stone couldn't possibly want her to end up with him. Right?

It had to be a test of some sort. Or a cruel cosmic joke if he was indeed the man she was destined to marry. For she could see no way of that happening with her family's blessing.

Unhappy with this awareness, she tried not to think of the dreams invading her mind every night. They consisted of moonlit walks, the gentle touch of his hand, a warm embrace, and the most remarkable kisses, so real Lilli felt as though they'd actually happened. Which had only increased her desire to seek out Mr. Henley and prove to herself she was making more of their brief encounter than what was reasonable.

But then he'd arrived at the stables, handsomely attired in dove grey breeches, black boots, and a perfectly tailored navy blue jacket. A few stray locks had caressed his brow with a carefree abandon that instantly sent her pulse racing. And just like that, she'd realized the pull she'd initially felt toward him had not been imagined. Nor had it lessened. If anything, it had transformed into a ravenous hunger she'd no clue how to appease.

So she'd averted her gaze for the sake of self–preservation and had left both him and her brother behind as soon as she got the chance. But she couldn't ignore Mr. Henley forever. Eventually she'd have to face him, or risk the uncomfortable questioning she knew she'd receive from her brother.

With this in mind, she drew Nora to a sharp halt when she reached the ruin of an old mill. The structure had been abandoned before she was born, when a damn built on a larger river several miles north had affected the water supply. Now, with the roof long gone and the mill wheel rotted away, the remaining structure was largely overgrown by vines.

Lilli swung from her saddle and collected a carrot from the bag of supplies she always carried during her rides. She snapped it in half and was feeding it to Nora when Henry and Mr. Henley arrived. Her stomach tightened and her skin grew hot on account of his presence.

"Not fair," Henry chided with humor, his voice a little throaty from exertion. "You know I can outride you if I'm given fair warning."

"Really?" Lilli focused her full attention on Henry in an attempt to ignore the havoc Mr. Henley played on her nerves. It was of little use. Her stomach was still in knots while her heart bounced about like an unhinged rabbit. Even so, she lifted her chin and casually asked, "Where is the evidence?"

Henry shook his head with a grin. "One day you and I will have to engage in a fair race with witnesses present."

"I'll still beat you," she answered with a smile wrought from pleasure. She did enjoy sparring with him.

"We'll see," Henry said with the confidence of a man who knew he was right.

Lilli did too. If her brother put in the effort and they began at the same time, she was fairly certain he'd outrun her with ease if for no other reason than having a horse superior to her own. Not that she would give Nora up for anything in the world.

"I'm not so certain," said Mr. Henley, the thoughtful gentility of his voice sliding down Lilli's spine with a silky smoothness that scattered tiny shivers across her shoulders. "Your sister's horsemanship is impressive, her seat so confident she looked at one with her beast. Forgive me for saying this, my lord, but if you were to compete against her with the same horse, I have an inkling she might win."

"First of all," Henry said, his attention on Mr. Henley, "we've recently established that you and I are friends. As such, I must insist you call me Henry. And second, aren't you supposed to be on my side?"

A smile pulled at Mr. Henley's lips, easing his features and turning him even more handsome than he'd been before. Lilli's pulse quickened even as she tried to deny the warmth she found in his twinkling eyes, to explain away her reaction with some sort of logical reasoning. Like the fact he'd helped her when they'd initially met even though he'd been the cause of her mishap in the first place, or how she'd been looking for a match because of the stone and had thus created the attraction in her own mind.

"That depends on whether or not you value honesty," Mr. Henley said in response to Henry's question.

"Which you know full well is a quality I insist upon." Henry huffed an exaggerated breath. Eyes dancing with humor he glanced at Lilli. "Perhaps it would be best if we refrained from racing. For the sake of preserving my pride."

He tossed Mr. Henley a blanket he'd snatched from behind his saddle. "Spread that out over there, would you? I'll bring some wine and a snack for us to enjoy while we relax."

～

Having come to terms with the fact that there was no avoiding Lady Lilliana today, Tristan permitted himself to indulge in the chance he'd been given to share her company. As unwise as this might be, he dreaded the notion of Henry discovering the interest he harbored for his sister. So he had to act naturally, which meant engaging in conversation as if all were as it should be, as if he weren't dying to haul Lady Lilliana into his lap and explore every inch of exposed skin with kisses. Consequences be damned.

A sigh raked his lungs while he idly lounged on one side of the blanket and listened to Henry's story regarding a hay cart his sister once stole. It was unheard of for a valet to be permitted such freedom. But since Henry had declared Tristan his friend, the barrier one would expect to find between a master and servant had, to some degree, been set aside.

"I borrowed it," she declared with an indignation that made Tristan's fingers burn with a fierce desire to touch her. He took a bite of the still-warm bread-roll Henry had given him. "There is a difference, you know."

"True. And I'm sure Mr. Oats would have agreed had you returned the cart in one piece," Henry remarked. "But it looked more like a pile of kindling than a cart by the time you were through with it."

"Only because I lost my grip on it while unfastening it from the goats."

"You used goats to pull a hay cart?" Tristan asked, sitting up straighter.

Lady Lilliana rolled her eyes. "I was twelve and

there weren't any other animals about. Certainly none I could manage on my own."

"You could have taken a wheelbarrow," Henry murmured. Lady Lilliana shot him a quelling look.

"What did you need the cart for anyway?" Tristan asked with increased interest. "And why would you take it from Mr. Oats?"

"Mr. Oats was the groundskeeper at the time, so it wasn't like I was trespassing." She slanted a critical look at her brother, no doubt because he'd made it sound as if Mr. Oats were a nearby farmer and she'd snuck into his barn. "Besides. I needed some means of transportation for Tabby and her kittens."

"Kittens?" Tristan prompted when Lady Lilliana failed to elaborate.

"My sister may have a history of getting into scrapes," Henry said with brotherly affection, "but she's also got a heart of gold. So when she discovered one of our cats had given birth in a field, leaving her and her litter exposed to predators, Lilli grabbed the cart and transferred them to our barn."

"But there's a steep hill behind the groundskeeper's cottage," Lady Lilliana said, her gaze averted and her cheeks a deep shade of pink, "so when I went to return the cart, it rolled away from me and smashed against a tree."

The ridiculousness of the story and the imagery it evoked, coupled with Lady Lilliana's almost bashful telling of it, caused amusement to rise within Tristan. It bubbled and grew, expanding up through his throat until it burst past his lips in a most undignified laugh. His shoulders shook and his eyes began to water.

"I can only imagine how you must have looked–" he coughed, aware Henry was laughing as well "–standing there–" he sucked in a breath and attempted to temper his mirth "–with two goats, abandoned by a runaway cart."

"It's not funny," Lady Lilliana said though Tristan detected a chuckle in her voice.

He met her gaze and deliberately held it. "I beg to differ, my lady. In truth, I cannot recall a more diverting story."

"In that case," she said, a smirk of mischief playing along the edge of her glorious mouth, "I should tell you about the time Henry returned home without his shoes."

"Don't you dare," Henry warned, albeit with good–natured cheer.

Eyes sparkling with the sort of malevolent delight only a sibling can manage, Lady Lilliana dove straight into her story, which Henry corrected at least a dozen times while claiming her version was highly exaggerated.

Tristan absorbed every word with the sort of pleasure one receives from a warm fire on a chilly night or a piece of decadent chocolate. Never in his life had he experienced such a state of pure comfort and harmony from another person's company. It occurred to him that while this was every bit the hoydenish trouble-maker he'd determined to steer clear of, now that he'd met Lady Lilliana, spent a few hours in her company, he couldn't imagine not seeing her again.

It was madness, to be sure. Inexplicable in every way. But dash it all, he wanted to spend more time with her, craved being able to witness her smiles and that bright light of mischief that shone in her eyes when she spoke of past exploits.

Most of all, he wanted to be alone with her, and as unwise as he knew it would be, he decided to find a way. As luck would have it, the viscount presented the perfect opportunity a few stories later when he declared a need to attend to nature's call. Rising, he told Tristan brusquely to keep an eye on his sister before he strolled away in the direction of the dilapidated mill.

Tristan looked at Lady Lilliana, his heart a frantic mess of unsteady beats. Her hazel eyes widened ever so slightly as if it had not occurred to her until now that they had been left without chaperone.

Intent on avoiding an awkward silence in the wake of the fluid banter they'd recently engaged in, Tristan asked, "How's your leg?"

"Perfectly fine. I only suffered a brief ache which was gone the next day." She leaned forward slightly, hesitated briefly, then murmured, "I'm glad you didn't fashion a crossbow to fire in response to a trip–wire or I might not be so forgiving."

Despite the jest, a shudder raked Tristan's spine at the thought of any harm coming to her. In fact, he felt a surge of protectiveness so fierce he vowed then and there that his trap–building days were over. If Henry wanted a rabbit for supper in the future, Tristan would ask the gamekeeper to provide it.

Deciding to keep the conversation light, he latched on to her comment and quietly asked, "You do not harbor ill feelings toward me then?"

"No."

Lord help him but there was a world of information in that one word, so simply spoken yet with an underlying edge of complication that spoke of despair, frustration, and longing.

However unwise, Tristan chose to explore it, if only so he'd have the memory of this day to look back on later, a secret pocket in time for him to savor once they parted and she went off to marry a suitable suitor.

"I realize I shouldn't be telling you this—"

"Then don't," she blurted, concern and possibly fear now evident in her expression.

Tristan shook his head. "You do not strike me as a coward."

"I don't consider myself to be one but…"

When she failed to continue Tristan impulsively reached for her hand, raised it to his lips, and placed a reverent kiss on her knuckles while steadily holding her gaze. Her lips parted on a whisper of breath while her eyes grew impossibly wide with surprise. Perhaps because of his inappropriate forwardness or, he hoped, because she felt the same simmering spark he did pulling at every nerve.

The kiss to her hand took no more than a second, upon which he swiftly released her and leaned back to add appropriate distance between them.

"I daresay there is more in heaven and earth, Lady Lilliana, than is dreamt of in any philosophy."

She swallowed audibly and appeared to clench her jaw while staring at him as if in quiet outrage. And then she stood with sudden abruptness. Without looking at Tristan, she addressed her brother who was now returning. "Henry, I think I'll leave you and your valet to enjoy the rest of the day together. I'm heading home so I can be ready for Grandmama's arrival."

Tristan knew Theodora Atwood, the Dowager Countess of Birchwood, was coming to join the family retreat which Lady Lilliana now chose to use as an excuse to quit his company. It stung, though not nearly as much as her use of *valet* instead of his name – an obvious attempt to put him in his serviceable place.

"If you'll just wait a few minutes," Henry said, "we can…" He huffed a breath as his sister leapt onto her horse and began her homeward trek without a backward glance. "As much as I love her, I pity the man she'll eventually marry. Heaven knows the poor sod will have his work cut out for him reining her in."

Tristan said nothing. In his opinion it would be a pity to try and restrain Lady Lillian's spirit. Furthermore, he wouldn't mind being the poor sod Henry referred to. On the contrary, he'd count himself a lucky bastard indeed if he had even one chance in hell of making her his.

# CHAPTER FOUR

Lilli paced her bedchamber while sorting through her turbulent thoughts and emotions. After returning from her ride she'd ordered a hot bath, hoping this would help her relax. Instead, sitting still had only made her more restless.

Now, dressed in a sage green day dress she'd put on in preparation for Grandmama's visit – not because she knew the color suited her and she hoped Mr. Henley might see her in it – she tried to figure out what to do. Not only with herself but with the unwelcome sensations her brother's employee managed to coax from her.

When he'd clasped her hand sparks had ignited deep in her stomach. And when his lips had brushed over her skin…

Gasping for breath, Lilli drew to a halt and placed one palm against the window overlooking the front driveway. Leaning forward, she pressed her warm cheek against the cool glass in an effort to stop the feverish effect the memory wrought on her body.

How dare he quote Shakespeare of all things? How dare he increase her interest by doing so?

She closed her eyes briefly and inhaled deeply, slowly forcing her heart into steadier beats.

She reached up idly and folded one hand around the quartz pendant. "Why are you doing this to me?"

The whispered words had scarcely been spoken before she spotted a carriage. Lilli watched its approach with quiet relief. Grandmama was finally here, providing Lilli with the opportunity to get the answers she needed.

Of course she had to wait for the lady to be received by her parents, which involved a much too long conversation over the most tedious tea–drinking Lilli had ever endured. After which the dowager countess declared her intention to take a nap because the journey had worn her out. Lilli forced back a groan and resigned herself to additional waiting.

By five o'clock she believed herself ready for Bedlam. Having perched on a hallway bench with a clear view of her grandmother's door, Lilli tried to pass the time with a book even though it was nearly impossible to focus on the plot. The words seemed to dance across the page in a nonsensical tangle of ideas she had no hope of absorbing.

Finally, after what felt like an utter eternity even though the hallway clock suggested only one hour had passed, the door to her grandmother's room opened.

Lilli shot to her feet, dropping her book in the

process and causing her grandmother's maid, Tabitha, to turn in surprise. "Good afternoon, my lady."

"Good afternoon." When Tabitha's gaze took in the book on the floor, Lilli stooped to pick it up. Swallowing, she clutched it between her hands. "Is the dowager countess awake?"

"She is." Tabitha inclined her head. "Shall I inform her you desire to speak with her?"

Lilli nodded. "Please do."

No more than a minute passed before she was ushered into the bedchamber. Her grandmother gave her one look before swiftly dismissing the maid. The door closed and Grandmama held out her hand, urging Lilli closer to the chair in which she reclined. Her forest green eyes studied her closely as she approached.

"What's troubling you, my dear?"

A long and heavy sigh pushed its way up Lillian's throat. She took the outstretched hand and held on tightly. "I…"

There was suddenly too much to say, too many forceful emotions all leading to too many questions.

Grandmama nodded toward a chair adjacent to her own. "Why don't you sit and calm yourself. I'm sure whatever the issue is, you and I will manage to find a solution."

Comforted by the gentle tone, Lilli lowered herself to the cushioned seat. Although Grandmama said nothing further, the ensuing silence was filled with expectation.

Lilli allowed herself a moment to clear her head

before saying, "I don't think the rose quartz crystal is working."

Her grandmother appeared to mull this over. She gave Lilli a speculative glance. "Were you not the first of my granddaughters to suggest this, I might believe you and chalk up to coincidence my own accomplishment with the crystal all those years ago. But you've seen the success your three cousins had in making love matches this past year. Perhaps it is simply taking you longer to find your intended."

"The problem isn't so much in not finding him," Lilli confessed, "but rather with his being absolutely and totally…" She waved her hands as if that would explain her predicament.

"What?"

Lilli groaned. "I think I might be destined to end up with Henry's valet, Mr. Henley."

Grandmama leaned back. Lips pursed and eyes wide she looked like a startled fish. A very short, "Oh," was her only response before she eventually knit her brow and asked, "are you sure?"

"No. Of course not. That's why I think there must be some mistake."

"Hmm…"

Her grandmother's pensive tone didn't offer the reassurance Lilli had hoped to find by confiding in her. "I mean" – she laughed, but it sounded nervous instead of dismissive – "an earl's daughter cannot possibly marry a servant. Can she?"

Rather than answer the question, Grandmama folded her hands in her lap as if they were merely discussing the latest novels they'd read. "Tell me, what was your first encounter with Mr. Henley like?"

"He rescued me," Lilli said. "From a rabbit trap he himself had dug."

Grandmama chuckled. "And?"

Lilli didn't pretend not to know what her grandmother asked. "It was as though time stood still the moment I saw him, and then, when he knelt to pull my leg from the hole, the touch of his hands, his nearness and scent, awoke something so fundamental to my existence I feared I might die when he released me." Realizing she was gripping her armrest, Lilli forced herself to relax her fingers. "This need for added closeness with him has been getting worse ever since."

"And it won't get any better until you accept it for what it is."

Lilli shook her head. "How can I? The situation is utterly impossible."

"Challenges are to be expected, and since you and Mr. Henley are clearly destined to be together, there must be a way to overcome this particular one. Tell me, what do you know of his background?"

"He mentioned having two younger sisters when Henry and I went out riding with him earlier today."

"And his parents?"

Lilli blinked. "I've no idea."

"Well then." Grandmama stood. "I recommend we do some research. I'll start by quizzing your brother over dinner."

"You think Mr. Henley might be more than what he appears?"

"I've no idea, my girl, but if he is then that would certainly solve your problem. Wouldn't it?"

Since her grandmother made a valid point and she was hopeful her reasoning would prove correct, Lilli gave her a quick hug, thanked her, and went to prepare for dinner.

The ebbing days of summer provided the perfect climate for a picnic, and today's mild afternoon sun warmed the otherwise cool air. Guests had begun arriving an hour ago, filling each corner of Stratham Hall with an insufferable buzzing that grated on Tristan's nerves. Thankfully, they'd all disappeared outside to sit on blankets near the pond while eating sandwiches and cake, leaving the indoors blissfully silent.

Even so, it was impossible for Tristan to enjoy the reprieve when he looked out the window and saw no fewer than five young gentlemen showering Lady Lilliana with attention. At this distance he couldn't gauge her response, not that it mattered when he knew each one would make her a far better match than himself.

Vexed by this, by the inferiority imposed upon him due to his father's actions, Tristan turned his back on the bothersome scenery and decided to go for a walk. He needed to move, to expel the tension building inside him. To focus his mind on something besides the woman he could not have. If at all possible.

Besides, nothing constructive would come of

standing about worrying over something he had no control over. So he strode along the paved edge of the long rectangular water features dug into the left side of the garden. A neat row of conifer trees shielded him to some degree from anyone glancing his way.

Heels clicking against the paving, Tristan crossed between two of the water features and descended a series of stone steps leading toward the flower garden. Here, tightly trimmed hedges marked the edges of winding pathways intended to take the visitor on a fragrant journey of colorful exploration. There were benches too, placed in carefully designed square areas intended to link each path, allowing for plenty of opportunity to sit and enjoy the surrounding beauty.

Tristan inhaled deeply, then pushed the air back out, and felt some of his tension abate. The sound of gravel crunching beneath his boots accompanied him as he proceeded at a more leisurely pace. It was peaceful here, a sanctuary for any chaotic mind. He almost regretted not bringing a book when he sank down onto one of the benches a short while later.

A couple of sparrows hopped around near his feet while butterflies and bumblebees flew with lazy abandon between the asters and dahlias that filled the surrounding flowerbeds. Relaxed, Tristan let his mind wander. He thought of how lucky he was to have found employment with Henry, who'd taken him on right away despite his lack of references. He considered his sisters, Iris and Emma, whom he'd been forced to leave behind with his parents.

Heavy regret weighed upon him as he recalled the

tears Iris had bravely tried to hide when they'd parted. Although she'd reached her sixteenth year, Tristan still thought of her as a child when compared to his own age of five and twenty. Yet she was the eldest now living at home and as such, Emma would look to her for guidance and for protection against their father's frustrated outbursts.

Unfortunately, neither she nor Iris had been the spares Papa had hoped for. And he wasted no time informing them of the fact that they were a burden.

From what Tristan gathered, conceiving had been no simple task for Mama. There had been numerous miscarriages. Tristan's own birth had been difficult. But then, nine years after he'd entered the world, he'd been blessed with a sister.

He'd never forget Papa's reaction when he'd learned he'd fathered a daughter instead of a son.

"She'll bleed us dry, that one."

Tristan had stared at Papa with incomprehension. "What do you mean?"

A snort had preceded a swift swig of brandy. "Expectations must be met."

Tristan hadn't understood at the time. Six years later, when Emma was born, he'd been old enough to comprehend the weight a daughter could place on a family. But he'd not realized his father struggled to balance the books or that the need to produce not one but two dowries after paying for Eton and Oxford kept him up most nights.

During his childhood and adolescence, Tristan had lived with the illusion of being well-off. But with more money exiting the family account than being added to it, poverty was an eventuality he'd not been aware of until suspicion had prompted him to check Papa's ledgers.

When he'd been caught, a massive row had ensued. It had led to Tristan's departure, though not without the assurance that he would find a way to solve the family's financial dilemma and that funds would soon follow.

Papa had told him he didn't need assistance, but according to the letters Tristan received from Mama, the money he provided was put to good use.

The sound of crunching gravel scattered his thoughts and drew his attention to the left. His heart jolted at the sight of Lady Lilliana strolling toward him with her grandmother.

A series of conflicting emotions assailed him. On one hand, he was ridiculously pleased to have her intrude upon his solitude. On the other, he was frustrated to no end.

He'd come here to escape her and the fierce desire he felt at her nearness. She caused his every nerve to stand on end and made his heart trip over. Even something as simple as breathing became a problem he was sure only she could solve by pressing her mouth to his.

*Madness.*

Feeling and thinking this way was sure to drive him insane.

He stood, ready to greet her and the dowager countess.

"Good afternoon, Mr. Henley" said the countess. "I

see you've had the same idea as us in coming here. I hope we're not intruding."

"Not at all." Unable to resist, Tristan looked directly at Lady Lilliana and experienced an immediate surge of pleasure when he noted her blush. "Your company is greatly appreciated."

"Indeed," the countess murmured while the color in Lady Lilliana's cheeks deepened. "You won't mind if I sit then? I fear these old legs of mine won't carry me back to the house unless they rest for a while first."

The old woman followed this remark by visibly slumping as though she might fall at any second. Tristan rushed forward and wound one arm around her waist in an effort to hold her upright. Which, he belatedly realized, wasn't the thing to do when assisting an elderly peeress one wasn't well acquainted with.

Too late to worry about that now he decided, guiding her to the bench. She sank onto the stone seat with surprisingly little aid from him.

*Hmm...*

"Are you all right?" Lady Lilliana asked the countess with marked concern. She'd crossed to where she sat and was now holding her hand. A mixture of affection and concern crinkled the edges of her eyes and filled Tristan's heart with warmth. This woman was so much more than a boisterous hoyden. She was also extremely caring.

"Perfectly so, my dear. Please don't trouble yourself about me. Instead, you should let Mr. Henley show you the roses."

Lady Lilliana frowned. "You look very pale, Grandmama. I'm really not sure I should leave your side."

Tristan's heart dropped. The countess seemed perfectly fine with plenty of color in her cheeks as far as he could tell. Which had to mean that Lady Lilliana was trying to find an excuse not to spend time alone with him.

It was the wise course of action he supposed, not entirely dissimilar to the excuses he'd been employing since he'd met her. But damn it all, this opportunity her grandmother was creating for only heaven knew what reason was not to be squandered.

Squaring his shoulders, he took a step forward and offered Lady Lilliana his arm. "Come, take a walk with me while her ladyship recovers."

Lady Lilliana stared at him, then at her grandmother. "But–"

"Go on," said the dowager countess. She'd already closed her eyes. "I want to enjoy the birdsong."

Lady Lilliana pressed her lips together in a firm line. She clearly didn't approve of how she was being managed. Eventually she huffed a breath and latched onto Tristan, singeing him with the touch of her hand, despite its being gloved. His muscles flexed in response and that was when he heard her gasp. Not loudly, but enough for him to know he wasn't the only one affected by their closeness.

A smile tugged at his lips as he guided her farther away from their chaperone. Daring a glance in Lady Lilliana's direction, he noted the high color in her cheeks, accentuated by the golden rays of afternoon sun. Her lips, a deep pink shade, were made for kissing, for sliding over hot skin with velvety softness and…

He jerked his gaze back to the flowerbeds and cleared his throat. "Are you enjoying the picnic, my lady?"

They walked a few paces in silence before she surprised him by saying, "Not really."

A startled laugh pushed its way up his throat. "No? I thought such diversion appealed to most ladies."

"Apparently, I'm different from the norm. Though I must confess the picnic was my idea."

He glanced at her again and saw a distinct look of concern in her eyes. Slowing his pace, he carefully asked, "Why would you plan an event you're not interested in?"

"Because…" She met his gaze then and all he could think of was how troubled she looked. There was a deep-rooted panic about her he dearly wanted to smash to pieces until she'd no worries left. "It was to be a distraction, but the people who showed up were so annoyingly eager to outdo each other with stories of their own accomplishments. The gentlemen especially. And all I could think about the entire time was…"

"Yes?"

She knit her brow and to Tristan's eternal frustration, chose to direct the conversation elsewhere rather than finish her sentence. "Let's talk about something else. Like you and your family. If I recall, you have two sisters?"

"Indeed I do," Tristan said, guiding her down a path that led straight to a rich display of roses.

"How old are they?" Interest softened her tone and caused Tristan's heart to swell.

"Sixteen and ten. Iris, the elder of the two, is a lovely young woman though a tad too timid. Emma on the other hand is more outgoing."

"You speak of them with fondness," Lady Lilliana noted. "You miss them?"

"Yes." The confession forced him to face the dread always lurching about in his gut. "I'm hoping to help them improve their prospects with my earnings. If I can give them a choice when it comes to marriage, I'd be satisfied knowing I've done my duty."

"I trust your parents are no longer with you then?" Before Tristan could answer she said, "That must be incredibly hard on you. I mean, the responsibility you must feel is one I cannot relate to. I admire any man who is willing to do what he can for his relations. Life can be difficult. Especially for women."

"You're not wrong, but you misunderstand me. You see, my parents are still alive and, well... It is just..." Shame poured through him at the thought of admitting what he'd not revealed to another soul, not even to Henry. But he'd always prided himself on honesty so allowing Lady Lilliana to think his parents were dead when they weren't did not sit well with him. "My father cannot seem to hold on to his money."

"Oh."

Tristan bit back a curse and averted his gaze while heat swept the length of his spine. *Well done.* If his intention was to push her away then making himself look pathetic would surely prove effective.

To his surprise, Lady Lilliana drew closer to his side and gripped his arm a bit tighter. "That doesn't lessen the burden you carry or the respect I have for your determination to do right by your sisters," she said. "Indeed, I would think that having an irresponsible parent one cannot rely on is harder than not having any." She sucked in a breath. "Forgive me. That sounded much better in my head than spoken out loud. How callous you must think me."

"Not in the least." He halted, then turned to face her. "Indeed, I think you're the loveliest woman I've ever encountered."

The pink in her cheeks deepened. "Would you think me too forward if I were to tell you I hold you in a similar regard?"

Her words were like sunshine warming his skin. "Not at all. I'd keep the compliment close to my heart forever."

A soft vulnerability filled her eyes before a wicked gleam replaced it. "What's the most embarrassing thing you've ever done, Mr. Henley?"

The question caught him by surprise so he had to think on it for a moment, until he recalled an incident from his childhood. "When I was a boy, about nine or ten, I was playing with other lads after church while our parents socialized over tea at the vicarage. At some point one of the older boys began boasting about having read *Fanny Hill*."

"Goodness."

He glanced at her in surprise. "You know of it?"

"I may or may not have snuck a peek at Henry's

edition," she confessed with a blush. "Promise you won't tell him?"

"Your secret's safe with me," he assured her.

Her features relaxed. "So then what happened?"

He shrugged one shoulder. "The other boys chimed in about having read it as well. I didn't want to be the odd one out, so I told them I'd read it too without any clue as to what the book was about."

"Oh dear." Even though she appeared to be making a stoic attempt at looking serious, her lips twitched with humor.

He gave her a quelling look. "Naturally the boys quizzed me. They asked me which part I liked the best."

"And what did you say?"

Tristan let his own lips slide into a smile. "The part about the hill."

Lady Lilliana burst out laughing in the most unladylike manner. Her whole body shook while tears spilled from her eyes. And then she snorted and all Tristan could think of was how much he wanted to pull all that joyful energy into his arms.

"How about you?" he asked instead. "What was your most embarrassing experience?"

She swiped at her damp cheeks and gulped down a series of breaths before telling him, "I vomited in the Duchess of Merryweather's vase once."

Tristan stared at her, aghast. "No."

"Oh yes." She sniffed, cleared her throat. "Mama and I were invited to visit the duchess last year for a ladies luncheon she was hosting. That morning at home, we were served eggs, bacon, pancakes, and custard–filled pastries to celebrate Papa's birthday. All of those dishes are favorites of mine, so I couldn't resist and foolishly overate. Then when we were shown into the duchess' parlor, the cloying scent of perfume from a dozen women caused my stomach to turn and before I knew it, I'd grabbed the nearest container and cast up my accounts."

"I suppose the duchess should have thanked you for saving her rug," Tristan said.

Lady Lilliana raised an eyebrow. "I was swiftly sent home to recuperate and neither I nor Mama have been invited back. It was not my proudest moment since I do tend to pride myself on having a robust constitution. But that smell…" She scrunched her nose. "It was nauseatingly sweet."

"Does your mother blame you for ruining a valuable connection?"

"No. Mama was lovely. She knew I didn't do it on purpose. Her primary focus was on me and making sure I was all right."

Tristan appreciated that since he was fairly certain his own mother would have been angered by the humiliation.

They walked a few paces before he asked, "What's the most outlandish thing you've ever done?"

She slanted her chin. "Probably swimming naked in the pond."

"And the most terrifying?" Tristan pressed while doing his damnedest not to linger on the image her most recent comment evoked.

"Facing you." Her honesty slayed him, but before he

could think of a suitable response, she spun away from him with a quipped, "Your turn."

Tristan inhaled deeply. He dropped his gaze to some coral–colored roses with yellow centers, more unique than any he'd ever seen before. Reaching out, he broke off a stem and twirled it between his fingers.

"I suppose the most outlandish thing I've ever done is pretend to be someone I wasn't."

She faced him again, her expression distinctly curious. "What on earth would compel you to do that?"

"It was the only way for me to acquire the job I wanted," he said, making his answer as truthful as possible.

She stared at him for a moment during which he feared she'd seen right through him. But then she gave a small shrug of her shoulders. "I can only assume you lacked the references but knew you had the qualifications."

"Precisely." Tristan offered the rose.

She took it without hesitation and raised it to her nose for a deep inhale before saying, "I imagine a lack of references can make it hard for capable people to gain employment, especially when their education ought to make them deserving of good positions. You quoted Shakespeare yesterday?"

"Indeed. I'm extremely fond of his plays."

"As am I." A sweet smile followed this statement before she turned serious. "Forgive me if this may seem ignorant, but I never imagined a working class man would favor such writing."

"Indeed, I've read most of the dramas, particularly

those that feature people who once existed since I've a penchant for history."

"I must confess, I've always found the subject horribly dull, with the exception of a few stories Henry once told me."

"I'm sure I can think of some interesting facts to boggle your mind, like how Napoleon Bonaparte was once attacked by bunnies."

Lady Lilliana laughed. "You're joking."

"Not in the least. Apparently a rabbit hunt went awry and the three thousand bunnies released for the occasion charged Napoleon and his men instead of running away."

"When was this?"

"1807. I'll never forget reading about it in the paper or seeing the caricature that went along with the article."

"So you keep abreast of current affairs as well?"

"I've been doing so since I was ten," he said without thinking. Noting her startled expression and fearing she might inquire about the extent of his education next, he quickly changed the subject. "Now ask me what my most terrifying experience has been."

When she did, he took a step closer to her while admiring the way the sun caught in her hair and made her skin glow. The pull was too great, a current he couldn't keep fighting.

So he leaned in slowly, allowing her all the time in the world to retreat as he answered her question with a whispered, "This."

*Good grief!*

Mr. Henley was kissing her out in the open and it felt wonderful – like a cool drink of water to quench her thirst on a hot summer's day or being warmed by a fire on a cold winter's eve. Electrifying and delicious came to mind too as she wound her arms around his neck and drew him closer.

A raspy groan vibrated through her from his mouth to hers as he pulled her tight against him and deepened the kiss. It was unlike anything Lilli had ever experienced – a communication of heart and soul on the most basic level.

As much as she'd tried to deny what was happening, this kiss confirmed every hope and every fear.

Mr. Henley was without a doubt the man for her. The joy he instilled in every fiber of her being was indisputable. With one simple glance he made her feel as though she were his every desire and with his kiss...

Sweet heaven, it was as though she were floating in a bubble of pure, undeniable bliss. The warmth of the sun against the nape of her neck was cooled by a late summer breeze. Birdsong sifted through the air, the light trill a perfect accompaniment to her heart.

Mr. Henley's hold on her tightened, encouraging her to sigh with pleasure as he kissed her with increased fervor. And then he withdrew, so suddenly he left her gasping.

"Forgive me. I could not resist." He stepped back, adding distance. A tortured expression tightened his features. "But I should have. To recklessly risk your reputation like that is completely inexcusable."

It was then that Lilli recalled their location. They were out in the open, visible to anyone else who happened along. Sucking in a breath, she glanced around, relief swamping her when she saw they were still alone, save for Grandmama whose eyes remained blessedly closed.

Heart thrumming and unsure what to do with her undeniable craving for more delicious kisses, Lilli swallowed and did her utmost to pull herself together. She'd always been the adventurous sort, ready to clamber into a tree, balance along a precarious ledge, or even hunt for game. But to throw herself into the arms of a servant without considering how such actions would affect not only her but her family was really too much.

Shaken by the experience and by what she knew she must do, she stiffened her spine and forced herself to meet Mr. Henley's gaze. She owed him at least that much. "You are not the only one at fault. I daresay I participated in equal measure, though I do believe it would be best if we pretended it never happened. It certainly cannot happen again."

Jaw tight, he gave a curt nod, then offered his arm without another word.

She took it and was once again overcome by an urgent need for added closeness. The instinct to press up against him more firmly, to inhale his scent and savor the heat of his touch was so fierce it took every strength she possessed to resist it. And somehow, despite the hot little shivers that darted up her arm with each move he made or the fact that her stomach had long since transformed into a giant butterfly, she managed to walk back to where Grandmama rested without instigating more kisses. As she was tempted to do.

"Shall we return to the picnic?" Grandmama asked once they'd parted ways with Mr. Henley a few moments later. He'd swiftly released her when they'd reached the bench, as though it pained him to touch her. After excusing himself, he'd stridden away at an angry pace.

Lilli couldn't blame him. She was rather vexed too and not the least bit pleased by the hollowness she experienced now in response to his absence. A lack of gratification accompanied the feeling, suggesting to her that there should be much more between them – that the kiss they'd shared was just the beginning.

Except it couldn't be.

"Lilli?"

Lilli blinked. What was it her grandmother had asked? Ah yes, the picnic. Exhaustion landed upon her shoulders at the prospect of having to entertain guests now. "I don't suppose we can avoid it, can we?"

Grandmama studied her carefully, until Lilli feared her face would catch fire. "Not when hosting it was your idea." She tilted her head. "What happened between you and Mr. Henley?"

"Nothing important."

The dowager countess snorted and started along the garden path at a dignified pace. "Liar."

With a choked cough Lilli fell into step beside her. "I beg your pardon?"

Her grandmother dropped a sardonic look in her direction. "There's a tortured sort of giddiness in your eyes, like you've just been allowed a taste of something you desperately want but cannot have." Her eyes sharpened and it was as though the ground opened up beneath Lilli. "He kissed you. Didn't he?"

"I...um...no?"

A full–bodied chuckle erupted from the dowager countess's throat. "Don't trouble yourself, my dear. Enjoy it. Savor it. Know that all is as it should be. It's just the stone working its magic."

Outraged by her grandmama's calm when Lilli felt like she'd been tossed straight into an apocalyptic typhoon, she halted, hands on hips, and glared at her. "How can you say such things when my chance of having a future with Mr. Henley is as absurd as sprouting wings and taking flight? I've said it before and I'll say it again, the stone must be wrong."

"Is that what it feels like to you?" Grandmama stared back at her with steely determination. "Forget the stone for a moment and focus on what your heart tells you. Is Mr. Henley the man you are destined to share your life with or not?"

Lilli's lips parted. She wanted to say he wasn't, but the words required to do so failed her. Eventually she expelled a weary breath and accepted the truth. "Yes."

The verbal admission lifted her spirit. She felt light, unburdened, for the first time since she'd realized who

Mr. Henley was and how difficult it would be for them to build a future together.

As if reading her mind her grandmother said, "Just because the stone has brought you together with your true love doesn't mean your journey will be easy. Mine wasn't. There were challenges to overcome. Papa was not of a mind to let a renowned rake court me. Reputations were at stake just as they are for you now. But facing these challenges and finding the courage to overcome them will make you all the more deserving of the ultimate prize."

"Risking scandal is no small thing. Papa would kill me. Mama too, I'll wager. This isn't just about me, it's also about them."

"Yes, it is. But their positions will withstand a great deal more than you realize. If it makes things easier for you, I can assure you of my support."

"Thank you. That means a great deal. But I'm still not sure I'm brave enough to take this on."

Her grandmother laughed. "Of all my granddaughters you are by far the most daring. Annie is known for her sweetness, Henrietta for her high spirits, and Eva for being a lovely romantic. But you're like a musket – unstoppable once your trigger's been pulled."

It was impossible for Lilli to keep from laughing. She still had concerns. Her head was filled with them, but her heart was lighter because of her grandmother's unrelenting belief in her. A thought struck as they resumed their stroll back to the house. "You orchestrated my meeting with him. Didn't you?"

Grandmama's lips twitched. "I may or may not have

noticed him heading toward this part of the garden. And I may or may not have invited you to walk with me immediately after."

"I suspect your sudden need to rest when we happened upon him was equally coincidental," Lilli murmured, albeit with an edge of amusement. "As was your suggestion I walk with him so you could enjoy your solitude."

Linking her arm with Lilli's, the dowager countess confided, "I may be old but I'm not obtuse. It would be hard enough for a titled gentleman to find the opportunity to further his acquaintance with you away from prying eyes. Being an employee, I realized Mr. Henley might need some help, so I decided to step in."

"Thank you." Lilli appreciated her doing so even if the encounter had only made matters harder for her. Because forgetting about Mr. Henley was no longer possible. Perhaps it never had been, but after being kissed by him she knew she could never share such an intimate moment with any other man. It would feel wrong and disloyal.

Which was properly stupid given the fact that no promises had been made between them. For God's sake, she'd known him for what, a week? And during that time they'd only spoken on three occasions, yet there could be no denying the strong connection she'd felt with him when she'd met his gaze for the very first time.

The comforting warmth he'd instilled in her breast, that need for added closeness and the overall feeling of rightness she had experienced in his presence, as though he were the missing piece to a puzzle she'd been attempting to solve her entire life could not be denied. Despite her attempts to do precisely that.

As she and her grandmother came within view of the picnic, Lilli drew a deep breath to bolster herself. She dreaded the turmoil the coming days and weeks would bring, but she knew deep down she'd have to face it. Because she would never forgive herself if she turned her back on Mr. Henley and the happily ever after she knew with certainty he could provide.

# CHAPTER FIVE

Tristan was in hell.

There simply wasn't any other way to describe the torture he was presently being subjected to. For two days he'd ridden with Henry, helped him with his correspondence, polished his boots and pressed all his clothes. Twice. He'd even taken to doing sums whenever he had a spare moment, since he'd been certain that focusing on the calculation of numbers was sure to drive a certain young lady from his mind.

It hadn't.

If anything, her constant presence in his thoughts made him an abysmal mathematician. He couldn't focus. All he could think of was her, the concern she'd shown toward her seemingly tired grandmother, the sympathy in her eyes when he'd spoken of Iris and Emma, and the exquisite press of her lips against his.

She'd felt so perfect in his arms, like a long lost piece of his heart that had finally found its way home.

*Stupid.*

He shook his head and glanced up from the ledger he'd been attempting to study and found Henry watching him from the doorway.

"Is everything all right?" Henry asked. He tilted his head and narrowed his gaze. "You look a bit odd. Like you're being tortured by a tasty cream puff you cannot have."

Tristan choked on a laugh and instantly wondered how Lady Lilliana would feel about being compared to a dessert. A mental image of her lying naked in his bed with her hair draped over his pillow assailed him with startling clarity. His pulse leapt and his gut tightened. Heat sank lower until sitting still became an uncomfortable chore.

All of this while her brother kept his gaze firmly upon him. Dear God. He'd turn into a raving lunatic if this continued. Embarrassed, he shifted and cleared his throat. "Forgive me. I cannot seem to focus today."

"Because you're still trying to figure out what my costume should be for the upcoming masquerade?"

"Precisely," Tristan said, latching onto the perfect excuse without hesitation. "Naturally, I want you to look your best."

Henry nodded and sauntered farther into the room. He approached one of the two spare armchairs and sat, legs stretched out and crossed at the ankles. "I still can't believe we're having a ball. Mama always tries to avoid hosting events while we're here because she feels there's enough fuss when she's in London. To her way of thinking our time spent here should be used for relaxation."

"I trust she wasn't the one to suggest it then?" Tristan asked.

"No. Grandmama did that. In fact, she insisted upon it so strongly I wondered if she might have some ulterior motive besides her excuse of wanting to relive her youth." Henry's brows drew together briefly before he raised his chin and looked directly at Tristan. "She inquired about you, by the way."

"What?" Apprehension pricked at the nape of Tristan's neck, washing his skin with an itchy heat.

"Wanted to know how you came to be in my employ. It was all rather odd. The interest on her part, I mean. Particularly with regard to your family."

Tristan's mind raced. He'd been careful thus far, hiding the truth from his employer, but if questions were being raised, there was a chance he'd soon be found out. And what would happen then? He'd not so much be sacked as politely asked to leave. Because if there was one thing he was certain the viscount wouldn't accept, it would be learning he'd hired a gentleman to see to his toilette and keep his affairs in order.

And yet, he did not want to lie. Not when they'd become friends and he genuinely liked and respected the man. So what the hell could he say?

"I told her your parents have fallen on hard times and that you're aiming to help them and your younger sisters, which is what you've told me. I hope you don't mind my sharing that information?"

Tristan blinked, relieved to realize he wouldn't have to say anything else. He shook his head. "No. It's the truth, after all."

Or as close to the truth as he was willing to go. Without a fortune or a title, his chances of winning an earl's daughter were nonexistent anyway. Best then to avoid letting the world know the Henleys were so desperate their son had been forced into service. To do so would only bring shame to the family name, and that wasn't something Tristan would do for any reason.

"I would recommend keeping it simple," Henry said.

"I beg your pardon?" Tristan asked, realizing belatedly that he must have missed a part of the conversation.

The apprehension in Henry's eyes suggested he might be worried Tristan had hit his head. "Regarding my costume for the masquerade?"

"Of course. Will black attire with a half mask do?"

"Splendidly so." Henry moved as though preparing to stand, only to settle back into his seat. "I almost forgot. Papa and I have been considering the gentlemen who participated in the picnic and have decided Mr. Ershwin and Mr. Newhurst would both make excellent suitors for Lilli. If you could, I'd appreciate your writing up a list of comparisons between them. Everything from their properties and annual incomes, to their ages, relations, and so forth. I especially want to know if there's any damning information about either one."

Tristan stared at Henry while doing his best to keep

his expression neutral. "In other words, I am to investigate them."

"Precisely," Henry remarked in a cheerful tone.

"If you'll forgive me for saying so, is this task not better suited for your father's secretary? I am, after all, your valet."

"One who is more than capable of branching out, I've noticed." Henry jutted his chin at the ledgers. "Truth is, Mr. Phelps is related to Mr. Ershwin through marriage, so I fear for his objectivity. And besides, I trust you to make the right choice. If all goes well, Lilli will marry one of them at the beginning of next Season."

"But neither of these men holds a title," Tristan blurted.

"No, but we've tried all the ones who do and none was able to secure Lilli's consent. At least Mr. Ershwin and Mr. Newhurst are both young, handsome, and seemingly wealthy. My sister could do a great deal worse."

Tristan knew this was true. Lady Lilliana was in fact incredibly lucky to have a father as lenient as the earl. Not only did he permit her more freedom than most young ladies in her position enjoyed, he'd also allowed her time to find a life partner she approved of without insisting the man be a peer. But it was clear his patience was running out. The time had come for Lady Lilliana to pick her husband, apparently with Tristan's assistance.

He sat motionless at the desk long after Henry had quit the room. Just when he thought things couldn't get worse, he descended into the next level of hell.

"What are your thoughts on marrying for love?" Grandmama inquired loudly during dinner, causing Lilli's wine to go down the wrong way.

She sputtered and swiftly took another sip of her drink while her grandmother patiently waited for someone to answer her question.

Eventually Mama said, "We heartily approve as long as the match is a suitable one."

"Of course," Grandmama murmured. She sent Lilli the sort of defiant look that instantly put her on edge. That eagle–eyed gaze quickly shifted to Papa as she inquired, "But what exactly defines suitability?"

"You know the answer to that."

"And yet it's a subject I'd like to explore." Grandmama set her silverware aside while Lilli considered how she might slide from her chair and quietly disappear beneath the table.

"Very well," Papa said with a shrug. "I suppose suitability depends on the parties involved. For people of our set it has to do with rank, an unblemished name, one's financial situation and so on. If the parties happen to love one another, then so much the better."

Mama blushed. "Stratham and I were fortunate in that regard."

Warmth filled Papa's eyes as he smiled at her from across the table. "Indeed we were."

"As was I," said Grandmama. "But what if the person one falls for is not from one's set, so to speak? What if a baron's daughter, for example, desired to marry her father's coachman?"

The silence that followed was excruciatingly painful. Everyone gaped at the dowager countess. The food Lilli had just consumed rolled over in her stomach.

"What a preposterous notion," Mama said.

"Without a doubt," Papa murmured.

Across from Lilli, Henry frowned, which only made her want to leap from her seat and run from the room. Had he drawn the parallel and realized her interest in his valet? Or was he simply as stunned by Grandmama's question as everyone else?

"It would be nice if we lived in a world where such an association were possible," Henry eventually said. He spoke evenly, as though he were mulling the idea over in his head and gradually voicing his conclusions. "But the truth of the matter is we don't. A coachman could never marry a baron's daughter without consequence. For starters, their upbringing would be vastly different, so one would naturally wonder what they'd have in common and if it would even be possible for them to actually love one another. On this matter I would suggest that love would be an illusion based on attraction of a physical nature.

"Next, one might question whether a lady brought up in a grand home, accustomed to having servants, fine garments, carriages, and such, would be satisfied living on a coachman's salary. I think love matches are what we all desire, but I don't believe love is the only thing that matters."

"Well put," Papa said.

Lilli stared at her plate. Her meal was only half eaten but she could not bring herself to enjoy the rest. She'd not needed this discussion to know her choice would be difficult, but her family's words seemed to make it more impossible. It not only broke her heart, it also made her resent her grandmother for addressing the issue over dinner.

This should have waited until Lilli was ready.

"Now, regarding the masquerade you're having me host," Mama said, effectively changing the subject before her mother said anything more about inappropriate matches. "I'd like to agree on a guest list so I can send out invitations."

The conversation continued though Lilli failed to hear much of it. Her mind was elsewhere, most notably on a man who would be enjoying his dinner below stairs when he ought to be at her side. Disheartened by this thought, Lilli had no desire to sit with Mama and Grandmama in the parlor after dinner. So she excused herself and sought out the library instead. There she'd at least find a book to replace the one she'd finished earlier in the day.

The room was warm and inviting as she'd known it would be. The dark wood cabinetry, leather chairs, and blazing fire instantly soothed her distraught nerves. She'd always found sanctuary here as a child. Whenever she had received a scolding or she'd been mad at the world, the library had offered endless comfort and the escape she'd needed.

Her fingers trailed lazily over a familiar shelf – *her* shelf – where all her favorite books sat. Now was not the time for new novels she couldn't be certain would entertain her. But she didn't feel like Shakespeare either since that required a great deal of focus. And Daniel Defoe's adventure novels did not hold the same appeal as usual. So she paused when she reached her copy of *Sense and Sensibility*, confident the light romance would offer the perfect distraction. Tomorrow she would decide on a course of action. Most notably, she'd have to figure out how Mr. Henley might court her with her parents' permission.

It wouldn't be easy.

In fact, it would undoubtedly lead to conflict.

With a small huff of frustration, she settled into an armchair near the fire and opened the book to the spot where Marianne Dashwood meets Colonel Brandon for the first time. She read the text until she'd completed two pages, only to realize she couldn't recall a single word.

*Damn.*

She snapped the book shut and glared at the lively flames that were dancing in the fireplace. Focusing on anything besides Mr. Henley had become impossible. He was stuck in her head as firmly as her leg had been stuck in that blasted hole he'd dug.

Oh, if only her family hadn't decided to come here. If only Henry had chosen to head off to some other part of England with friends instead of bringing his dashing valet into her life. The complication her growing attraction toward him posed was well and truly the sort she would rather do without.

Raising her hand, she touched the quartz pendant and muttered a curse. She'd wished for true love to find her. She just hadn't thought it would turn her life upside down once it did.

A log snapped in the fireplace and then someone cleared their throat, bringing Lilli's attention toward the door and to the intensity of Mr. Henley's gaze. Her lungs drew tight and it suddenly felt as though every inch of her skin had begun to shimmer like morning dew sparkling beneath the early sun. Her breath caught next and whatever words she might have spoken lodged in her throat.

While she'd caught the occasional glimpse of him during the past few days, they'd not talked since their kiss in the garden. Partly because the opportunity to do so hadn't arisen. Mostly because she'd been a coward – too afraid of what was happening between them to run headfirst toward it – which was so unlike her. A fact that added to her vexation.

"Forgive me for intruding," he said, unmoving. "I did not expect to find anyone here at this hour."

"I came to relax with one of my favorite books, only to realize I can't. As it turns out, you've ruined it for me."

"I beg your pardon?"

With a sigh, she pushed her irritation aside and forced herself to hold his gaze, to be the fearless woman she'd always prided herself for being. "Why did you kiss me?"

He held himself completely still for the longest, most unbearable moment ever endured. After which he moved toward her, his gaze fixed upon her with unrelenting focus. Lilli's pulse raced and her stomach spun with dizzying speed. She clutched the armrest and prayed the chair would not collapse as easily as she would have done, had she been standing.

He halted at her side. His dark eyes snared her with the ease of a trained marksman, sending a series of hot shivers straight down her spine. Her toes curled in response even as her heart beat in eager anticipation of what he might say or do next.

"Because I had to."

The statement, so simple and honest, was beyond thrilling. She stared at him, unsure of how to respond. All she could think of was how much she longed to be held by him once more, to feel his lips against hers, his hands sliding over her skin. Even though they'd agreed it could never happen again.

She almost laughed. Who on earth were they trying to fool?

As if completely in tune with her feelings, he reached out and slid his fingers across her cheek with aching slowness. Sparks ignited in their path, pursuing them as he stroked down the side of her neck.

"Just as I have no choice but to touch you now," he whispered, his voice toying with every nerve ending in her body until she felt drugged. "I know this is wrong and I shouldn't want you, but the thing of it is—I do. More desperately than I want my next breath."

Lilli eased her hold on the armrest and leaned into his caress. "Would it make things easier if I told you I feel the same way?"

His fingers stilled. She heard him take a deep breath and expel it. "No. I daresay the only thing that would solve this problem is if you were to reprimand me for my forwardness or suggest to your brother he sack me."

She shook her head. "You ask the impossible."

"My lady, I–"

"Lilli," she insisted. "If you please."

He hesitated briefly, then he withdrew his hand, leaving a cool spot in its place. He retreated to the armchair adjacent to hers and shot her a wary glance before he eventually nodded. "Very well, Lilli. But only if you agree to call me Tristan when we're in private."

A surge of warmth filled her heart. "Of course."

The sheepish grin he gave her melted her insides until she felt like a gooey mess.

He jutted his chin at her lap. "What are you reading?"

A question that could lead to more appropriate conversation. This was good. But she still blinked and dropped her gaze to the book, having momentarily forgotten its title. She shook her head at her daftness and also because the effect Tristan had on her never ceased to astound her.

"*Sense and Sensibility*," she said. "It's rather good."

"I know," he said, surprising her.

"You do?"

His eyes twinkled with amusement while the edge of his mouth curved to form a crooked smile that made him look even more dashing. "It's a favorite of Iris's. She made such a fuss over it I eventually had to give it a go myself. And I'll admit, the plot and wit had me riveted from the first page."

Intrigued and quite frankly pleased beyond compare by his confession, Lilli leaned forward. "What did you think of Marianne's response to Colonel Brandon's attentions?"

"Honestly, I don't believe she deserved him until she'd grown as a person through her misadventure with Willoughby."

His answer satisfied her to no end. "Exactly so, though I do wish she'd appreciated him more from the start."

"Had that been the case, the plot would have been a bit thin, don't you think?"

"I do. It unfolds as it ought." She tilted her head. "What's your favorite book, if I may ask?"

"I suppose if I had to pick one it would be *The King of Pirates*."

"Excellent choice." She'd enjoyed the novel herself more than once and understood why such a tale would appeal to most men. "My copy is right over there alongside *Robinson Crusoe* and *Gulliver's Travels*. You're welcome to borrow any of the books the library has to offer."

"Thank you. Your brother made the same offer. But I actually came in search of something less entertaining. As unfortunate as that may be." His expression dimmed and Lilli's stomach dipped in response. "Your brother has tasked me with finding out more about Mr. Ershwin and Mr. Newhurst. I thought a history of the area and its families might be a good place to start. Provided such a text exists."

A cold chill slid down the back of Lilli's neck. "Henry imagines I'll marry one of them?"

"According to what he divulged, your father does too."

"Dear God." She stared at Tristan, at the painful regret in his gorgeous brown eyes and the unyielding straightness that stopped his mouth from smiling. A humorless laugh escaped her before she managed to school her features and give him an equally frank look. "I have no interest in Mr. Ershwin or Mr. Newhurst."

"Lilli." His voice was gentle, as though he were trying to soothe a child with a scraped knee. "Your Seasons have been unsuccessful, and if you'll forgive me for saying this, you are of an age where time is starting to be of the essence."

"And so I am meant to just settle?" she asked, unable to stop her voice from shaking. Her insides drew tight in anger. "How can I do that now, after meeting you?"

He held her gaze for the longest moment, the depth of emotion she saw in his eyes enough to make tears well in her own. Eventually he sighed. "You know as well as I do that we are impossible."

"I refuse to accept that. There simply has to be a way if it's what we both want." She sent him an imploring look. "Is it? What we both want, that is?"

"I think of you night and day," he admitted. "Truth is the magnetic pull I feel with you is unlike anything I've ever experienced before. With anyone."

"Then I shall continue with my plan."

His expression turned cautious. "Which is to do what, exactly?"

Raising her chin in an effort to combat the hopelessness nipping at her heels, she told him, "To gain Papa's understanding and blessing."

Tristan's eyes widened. "You're mad."

"Determined, more like."

"Lilli… Your father will never approve of you wedding a servant."

Warmth settled at the base of her spine and fanned up across her back, despite the bleakness of his words. She managed a coy smile. "I'm glad to know you're also thinking of marriage."

He leveled at her the most exasperated look she'd ever been subjected to, which was saying something. "Make no mistake. If I could, I'd start building my future with you tomorrow. Honestly, I don't know how my feelings for you have developed so fast. All I can say is there has been a connection between us right from the start, and the harder I try to ignore it, the stronger it grows."

"I feel exactly the same." If he was going to lay his heart bare then she would be equally brave. "Which is why I've made a decision."

"Go on," he said, with no small amount of wariness.

Straightening in her seat, she set her book aside on

a nearby table. "If Papa refuses to let me have you, we'll simply elope."

"Bloody hell." He gaped at her. "You're completely cracked in the head."

"I am no such thing." Indignation swept the breadth of her shoulders.

"Well, you certainly aren't thinking rationally," he insisted, his voice tight. "I am poor, in case that fact has escaped you. I have no means to support you." He stood so abruptly, Lilli jumped. His fingers raked through his hair and when he met her gaze, his eyes held a wild look that caused her pulse to race faster. "Your life is charmed— comfortable and easy compared with what you will face if you choose me."

"If you're trying to recommend yourself you're doing a terrible job," she offered dryly.

"I'm trying to do what's in your best interest."

"Stop." She pushed to her feet and glared at him. "My entire life has consisted of everyone trying to do what's in my best interest. I was forced to learn how to play the pianoforte. Even though I loathed every second. I was made to take tea with gentlemen callers I had no interest in. This may surprise you, but I actually happen to know what I want. And it's almost *never* what others believe to be in my best interest."

Her breath came hard and her face burned. Hands fisted at her sides, she stood, mere inches away from him, prepared to fight whatever retort he might give her.

Instead, he cradled her cheeks, and then his mouth was on hers. He kissed her with a hunger that matched her own. It was hard, almost violent, and so rough she could taste his frustration. Rather than deter her, it increased her need for added closeness and deeper contact. She raked her fingers through his thick hair, and inhaled his scent – a heady mixture of musk and pine.

His teeth scraped her lips as he pushed her backward, pressing her into a bookcase. She gasped, both from surprise and pleasure, and he instantly took advantage, plundering her mouth with an impassioned sort of brutality that marked her as his. It was wild and unapologetic – precisely what she craved. And when his hand gripped her thigh and he pushed his hips harder against her, newfound pleasure surged through her. She instantly shifted to give him more access.

This was better than anything she had ever experienced before. It was frantic, wicked, and utterly delicious. Hands roaming, exploring, mouths nibbling and tasting while sweet pressure grew inside her. A moan filled the air and…

Tristan froze.

His breaths were ragged, his heart a galloping mess. Heat scorched his back where Lilli's hands touched him—beneath both jacket and shirt. How the hell had that happened?

Warily, he opened his eyes and drew back a little, enough to see her dazed expression and her kiss-swollen lips. He swallowed and instinctively rolled his hips, making her shudder and sigh with such passion, his own arousal increased. And made it all the more difficult for him to do what he had to.

With a curse, he stepped back and added respectable distance. But there was nothing respectable about her ravished appearance or the too snug fit of his trousers.

Good God. He'd been on the verge of having his way with her in the library. With the door wide open. If that did not define insanity, he wasn't sure what did.

Knowing they could not be found here like this by anyone, he straightened himself and told her firmly, "You should go."

"But–"

"I still need to find the books I came for."

His words seemed to have the cooling effect he'd hoped for. She pushed away from the bookcase. A frown creased her brow. "So you're still going to help Papa and Henry gather information on Mr. Ershwin and Mr. Newhurst. After this?"

"It's my job, Lilli."

"Right. Of course." She smoothed her skirts and tucked some loose strands of hair behind her ears. Wordlessly, as though the act of speaking would tear her to pieces, she walked to the door. Her sweet fragrance of jasmine or some other floral scent assailed him as she passed, and nearly made him do something stupid like catch hold of her and kiss her again.

"You should get a costume." The comment was barely more than a whisper, delivered over her shoulder as she paused in the doorway. "At least then we'll be able to dance at the masquerade without anyone being the wiser."

It took a moment for him to follow her thoughts and recall the upcoming dance. His heart clenched at the idea of pretending just for one night that he was her equal. But what he feared most of all were additional interactions, each one strengthening the bond between them and making it harder for him to give her up. As logical reasoning told him he'd have to.

But before he could voice an objection, she swept from the room. He stared blankly at the closed door before he realized he was already trying to figure out what his costume should be.

Good Lord, she'd be the death of him.

Most likely with the aid of her father's pistol.

# CHAPTER SIX

The ballroom glowed with golden light spilling from hundreds of wax candles. Tristan had watched the footmen light them an hour ago. Now, standing in a far corner, he observed the swarm of guests from behind a golden mask that covered most of his face. Silks shimmered and jewels twinkled while champagne flowed. Dancing couples smiled and laughed as they moved in time to the lively tune being played.

Feeling like an imposter, Tristan held himself perfectly still. He hoped he'd avoid drawing attention while doing his best to convince himself that being here was a splendid idea and not a colossal mistake. But to leave after he'd caught a glimpse of Lilli had been impossible. A week had passed since their kiss in the library – a week filled with impassioned dreams he ought not be having and a burning desire to make each one real.

His heart thudded.

This evening she wore a white gown. Pleated in Grecian style, it hugged her slender figure in ways that ought to be illegal. It certainly made Tristan long to touch her, and to shove aside all the men he'd seen pay attention to her. She'd even danced with a few. Hell, she was dancing with one right now, holding her silver half mask in place with one hand while clasping her partner with the other.

The young man's palm settled neatly against the small of her back as he turned her around. His eyes glowed with satisfaction while an arrogant smirk pulled at his lips as he guided her through the various steps.

Tristan wanted to punch him.

His hands were already balled into fists.

With a growl, he took a step forward.

"If I may," said a masked man who suddenly barred Tristan's path, "I'd recommend *not* engaging."

Nervous energy settled in the pit of Tristan's stomach since there was no mistaking who this man was. He'd picked out his costume himself – had helped him dress for God's sake. Was it possible Henry had recognized him as well?

Feeling ill, Tristan did his best to simply breathe.

"Despite your excellent disguise, there's fury in your eyes and enough coiled tension in your body to fight off an army. But if you do, I'll have to have one of the footmen escort you out, which would make it impossible for you to keep an eye on the lady who's captured your heart." Henry shifted slightly so he had a view of the dance floor. "Which one is she?"

Feeling like a burglar who'd been caught with his hands full of loot, Tristan cast about for an answer that wouldn't see Henry strangle him. "The one in the red gown," he murmured, deliberately lowering his voice in a desperate attempt to maintain his ruse. Sweat had long since settled between his shoulder blades. He held his breath. Tried not to focus on the pounding of his heart, though it was so loud Henry would surely hear it.

"Mr. Hanover's wife?" Henry queried in an understandable tone of disbelief.

*Damn.*

"She um… That is to say… I, err…" If he could only untangle his stupid tongue, explaining himself would be so much simpler.

"No need to get into details with me," Henry said. "I know how the world works. I'm just surprised since I thought the Hanovers happily married. However, whether they are or not, one can't really fault the lady for dancing with her husband. You certainly can't barge over there and whisk her away from him. So here–" Henry handed Tristan a glass of champagne "–have a drink and bide your time. I'm sure the opportunity for you to dance with her yourself will arrive in due course."

"Thank you." Tristan practically sagged with relief as he grasped the proffered glass. He took a sip and savored the bubbly flavor, which had a wonderfully calming effect on his nerves.

"Ah look," Henry said a few minutes later, halting their discourse pertaining to the British army's continued presence in America. "Here's a pleasant distraction."

Tristan glanced in the direction Henry was looking and instantly lost all ability to think. All he could do was stand there and admire Lilli's beauty as she swept toward them. Her dark blonde locks fell in glorious curls around her heart–shaped face in a style only a masquerade would permit. His heart clenched as she drew to a halt before them. Pleasure poured through him the moment her eyes met his.

It lasted but a fraction of a second, yet it was enough to make every cell in his body tingle with fierce awareness. And need.

"Gentlemen," she said. Her attention settled on Henry. "You ought to be dancing. Indeed, I must insist you invite at least one of the ladies to partner with you for the next set."

"I was actually about to do so when I took the opportunity to stop an altercation between this fine fellow and poor Mr. Hanover," Henry said with an edge of humor.

"Indeed?" Lilli's questioning gaze found Tristan's once more. "I can't imagine why."

Henry leaned a bit closer to her and told her conspiratorially, "And it would probably be best if you didn't try to."

Tristan cleared his throat. He'd had enough of this misconception he'd caused and the risk remaining in Henry's company posed with regard to being discovered. It was time to find a way out of this tangle and into closer proximity with Lilli.

He executed a slight bow and gazed into her sparkling eyes. "If you are not otherwise engaged, perhaps you'd care to partner with me for the next set."

"What about Mrs. Hanover?" Henry asked. His voice held a teasing element

"She'll have to wait," Tristan said, his attention on Lilli.

"I'd be delighted," Lilli said. She moved closer and placed her hand on his arm.

It took tremendous effort for him not to hiss with pleasure as energy sparked to life at that point of contact. Swallowing, he drew her more firmly against him, then glanced at Henry. "Enjoy the rest of your evening, sir."

"Hold on a moment," Henry said as Tristan and Lilli started toward the dance floor. "I don't even know who you are and–"

"That is the beauty of masquerades," Lilli told him over her shoulder. To Tristan she added, "Let's hasten our stride. If we're lucky someone will intercept him before he catches up and demands an introduction."

"And if we're unlucky?"

"Worst case, you'll face him at dawn."

The comment was dire enough to make Tristan wonder if he'd made a terrible error in judgment by going along with Lilli's request, by kissing her not only once but twice, by courting scandal and risking her reputation. It was lunacy. But then a waltz started playing and he spun her onto the dance floor, and it was as if none of that mattered as long as he was able to hold her.

For now, he could dance with her in public. As if they belonged together. As if the rightness he felt as he held her could not be denied for any reason. As if she weren't a million miles above him in station. And in that moment every risk they took for the briefest shared pleasure felt as though it was totally worth it.

Lilli could scarcely believe her good fortune. She was dancing. Not with a rogue whose wandering hands had forced her to stomp on his foot at least once, but with Tristan in whose arms she felt both protected and cherished.

"You must forgive me," she said as he twirled her about. "I could not reach you sooner."

"I'll admit my patience was tested. I'll also confess to not liking the idea of you dancing with other men."

The harsh note of jealousy thrilled her in ridiculous measure. She beamed at him. "I rather think I'm the one who ought to take issue with you and your interest in a woman I know to be happily married."

He made a gruff sound and drew her closer. His hold on her tightened as he swept her past the orchestra with the skill of a man who'd clearly danced before. How positively curious.

"You know the only lady I care for is you," he murmured. "But Henry caught me off guard. I could hardly claim to be vexed on account of his sister."

"I suppose not," she said, unable to keep from smiling broadly. His stern expression had the most potent effect upon her. On one hand it made her giddy with knowing he didn't want other men anywhere near her while on the other it weakened her knees and filled her veins with liquid heat. "Thank you for coming, by the way. I feared you might decide not to."

"That would have been the prudent choice, but there's something about you that tempts me to be reckless." When she laughed, his frown deepened. "That's not a good thing, Lilli. It's the sort of thing that will lead to disaster."

"Or perfect bliss." When he said nothing, she pressed. "I mean to speak with Papa tomorrow."

"You're out of your mind."

Ignoring him she said, "He appreciates knowing that big decisions are well thought through, so I've made a presentation for him."

Tristan choked. "Seriously?"

"It offered the perfect distraction this week when I was unable to catch you alone. Which did make me wonder, by the way, if you were deliberately avoiding me once again."

He pressed his lips together and glanced away while steering her between two other couples. At the edge of the dance floor she spied her brother, who stood with his feet wide apart and arms crossed. His gaze followed her like a hawk. Oh dear. Apparently Henry disapproved of her dancing with a man who supposedly dallied with married women. And who could blame him?

"I've been kept busy with the matter I mentioned

last we met and with trying to find fault with Mr. Ershwin and Mr. Newhurst."

"And did you succeed?"

"No. Both men would make excellent matches for you from all points of view. I'm sorry."

Lilli's spirits dimmed somewhat though she was immensely grateful to him for trying to help her instead of Papa and Henry. "It's all right. As I mentioned, I've created a presentation just as I would have done if I wanted to open a charity or invest my savings in some venture."

"I fear you could easily prove a charity more lucrative than a future with me," Tristan grumbled. "No matter which way you turn it, I am a dismal option. You won't be able to tell Stratham otherwise."

"Let me try. Papa has always cared for his children's happiness, so I believe winning him over will be easier than you think." All she had to do was prove to him she wouldn't suffer in Tristan's care and that marrying him would not have a negative impact upon her family. As long as she caught Papa at the right moment, she was certain he'd listen. Or at least she hoped he would.

"What if this plan of yours blows up in your face? I'll be sacked without reference."

"Grandmama has already agreed to back me up. If I ask her to, I'm sure she'll give you another position." She squeezed his hand. "I'm simply aiming for the most agreeable outcome first, the one in which my family offers support and permits us to use my dowry to set up a home for ourselves."

He winced. "I'm not comfortable being dependent upon you."

"It would be no more than a practical start," she assured him. "If you wish to find other work so you can provide for us, I have no issue with that."

Shifting slightly as they slowed their pace in time with the fading music, he stared at her in amazement. "Truly?"

"You are a working man, Tristan. That's who I fell in love with. I've no intention of changing that."

He swallowed hard, as if it required great effort to rein in his emotions. His lips parted, but rather than speak he suddenly grabbed her upper arm and walked her briskly toward the edge of the dance floor.

"We need to talk. There's something about me you ought to know," he said, leading her out of the ballroom. "But your brother was approaching and he did not look the least bit pleased."

"I don't suppose he would after what you told him," Lilli said. She half walked, half ran in order to keep up with Tristan's much longer strides.

Without further comment he marched her toward the door leading into the music room and hauled her inside.

~

The door closed but Tristan remained on edge. He needed to be alone with Lilli so he could speak with her uninterrupted, but judging from Henry's clipped stride, rigid posture, and angry gaze, he feared his friend would burst in on them at any second. Taking Lilli's hand, he pulled her toward the glass door leading out to the garden. His heart beat rapidly, both with anxiety and with elation.

She'd told him she loved him, which had not only been unexpected but also incredibly welcome. It made the idea of fighting for a shared future with her less terrifying. Because it suddenly felt as though any other outcome would cause an imbalance in the cosmos. And who would want that?

They stepped outside, closed the door behind them, and descended the steps. From their right came the sound of laughter and chatter as guests enjoyed a reprieve on the terrace. Still holding Lilli's hand, Tristan drew her away from the house and deeper into the moonlit garden. He did not slow his pace until they'd returned to the spot where they'd shared their first kiss. Finally he halted, whisked off his mask, and pulled her into his arms.

Her own mask clattered to the ground as his mouth met hers with a hunger that rivaled their previous kisses. Because she loved him and he loved her, and he told her as much with every caress, with each fervent touch and the sighs of pleasure she wrought from his lips.

Turning, fumbling, he lowered himself to a nearby bench and pulled her into his lap. With a squeak she settled against him, her delicate hands framing his face as she pressed her mouth to his, feasting on him as though he were a treat she meant to devour.

Her passion fed his own, igniting the flames of his

ardor until he was desperate with need. Never in his life had he craved a woman as much as he craved Lilli. She was the air he breathed and the joy that gave his life meaning.

Guided by instinct, he tugged down the flimsy sleeves of her gown and kissed a path over the curve of her shoulder.

"I love you too," he whispered against her. "Fiercely. Wholeheartedly. Without apology." He punctuated each word with a kiss while travelling the edge of her décolletage. One hand found its way under her skirts, skimming her naked calf and thigh before settling boldly against her hip.

Moaning, she arched her back, offering herself in the most irresistible way. Hell, he could have been a monk and he'd still not be able to fight her temptation. So he dipped his head and allowed himself a taste of perfection.

The crunch of gravel stopped his heart.

It jolted back into a frantic rhythm as soon as he heard Henry's voice. "What the hell?"

Lilli gasped and Tristan tightened his hold on her body, gripping her while he tried to figure out what to do and, most importantly, what to say.

As the light from a lantern swept over them, Tristan experienced a falling sensation that warned him his life was about to change for the worse. He sucked in a breath and adjusted Lilli's gown while she clutched him with bruising force. Devil take it, he'd meant to talk to her, not ravish her. Least of all when he'd known her brother was in pursuit.

Where was his restraint and reasoning? Christ have mercy, he had to be the biggest imbecile ever to walk the earth.

"Unhand my daughter this instant," a deep voice growled.

Good God. Lilli's father had arrived too. Tristan gave Lilli a swift once over to make sure her body was respectably covered, then helped her out of his lap.

"It's all right," he whispered while mentally preparing himself to be skewered.

"Papa," Lilli said. Her voice was shrill and much too loud in the still evening air. "Henry. What an unexpected surprise."

Tristan nearly choked. Having risen as well, he stood by Lilli's side, ready to face the consequences of his actions. And prepared to defend her part in what would undoubtedly be viewed as a severe lack in judgment.

"What the devil possessed you," Stratham fumed. "Return to the house at once with your brother while I–"

"Papa," Henry clipped. "Mr. Henley is in my employ. As such, I am forced to bear some responsibility for his actions."

The stern look Tristan received from the man he'd counted a friend until now made him feel smaller than ever before – like a gnat beneath his shoe. Misery poured through him, yet he could not regret the kisses he'd shared with Lilli.

"If you would please allow me to handle this situation, Papa, I'd appreciate it."

The earl glared at Tristan for a long moment, his expression so murderous there was no doubt he was picturing Tristan's demise.

Eventually he nodded. "Come along, Lilliana."

"But I–"

"Now," her father snapped, "before I change my mind and decide to deal with Henley myself."

"Very well," Lilli muttered. To Tristan she whispered, "I'll find you later. We'll figure this out together."

"All right," Tristan said even though he doubted they'd have the chance. Not wanting to add to her troubles, however, he forced a smile to conceal his own heartbreak and watched as she walked away with her father.

"You've abused my trust," Henry said, his voice a blade of disappointment that cut Tristan to the marrow. "I treated you as my friend and this is how you repay me? By taking advantage of my sister?"

"I did not–"

"Enough!" Illuminated by the lantern he held in one hand, Henry's eyes glowed with demonic fury. "Don't you dare insult me by denying what I myself have just witnessed."

"Forgive me." Tristan stared at the man whose good favor he'd carelessly discarded. Regrettably, he knew he'd do it again if it meant having Lilli back in his arms. He squared his shoulders on this thought and told Henry firmly, "What you saw was no meaningless dalliance, however. I love her."

The shock on Henry's face was palpable. "Love her?" He spoke the words as though they were sour. "If that were true you would have her best interests at heart. You would not presume to imagine her future might lie with you."

"So what you're effectively saying," Tristan gritted, his own anger rising, "is that I am good enough to be your friend just not good enough to become your relation."

"You have the audacity to speak of marriage? With Lilliana?" Henry took a step closer to Tristan and leaned in, his features tight. "You are a servant. *My* servant, to be exact. You have no fortune, no house, no funds I'm aware of beyond what I've paid you, and no connections besides me and my family. So what, pray tell, can you offer an earl's daughter, besides a worse existence?"

It took every ounce of self-control Tristan possessed for him to maintain anonymity – to not reveal he was gentry and thus a more suitable match than Henry suspected. But what good would that do? He still wouldn't have the fortune Henry demanded, and the only house he could claim as one day becoming his own might be lost to the debt collectors unless he provided more funds.

As for connections, there was an aunt who'd married a baron, but she and her family kept their distance from Tristan's because of his father's financial misconduct. Tristan hadn't seen her since he was a child.

In short, there was nothing worth mentioning, nothing that might improve upon his situation. Indeed, confiding the truth could make matters worse since all it would do was prove he'd deceived Henry too, lied to him for months. It certainly wouldn't improve his chance of winning Lilli. If he'd had the tiniest inkling it might, he'd have done it.

Instead he said, "All I can offer is myself and the assurance that I will honor and protect Lilliana until my dying breath."

Henry held his gaze for a long, drawn out moment. Tristan's heart thumped so hard it actually pained him. And then Henry stepped back and spoke, his voice flat, "That's not enough."

Tristan knew this and yet it still felt like a punch to the gut.

"As distasteful as this is," Henry added, "I have to know if you've taken her innocence."

It was a reasonable question, given the circumstances, but it still made Tristan's insides twist with disgust. That Henry's opinion of him had fallen so low he imagined he'd ruin his sister thus, before she was married gutted him.

Somehow, he managed to hold Henry's gaze as he gave his answer. "I have not."

Henry expelled a heavy breath, the relief he showed like a boulder upon Tristan's shoulders. He slumped a little beneath the weight.

"Then there is nothing further for us to discuss," Henry said, his voice completely devoid of emotion. "Go to your quarters and pack your belongings. A carriage will be parked outside the servants' entrance within half an hour, ready to take you wherever you wish."

With that blunt statement, Henry turned and walked back to the house, leaving Tristan with a hollow sensation inside his chest. And as the darkness closed in around him, he cursed his heart for what it had caused him to lose.

# CHAPTER SEVEN

If there was one thing Lilli detested, it was being treated as though she were an incompetent child. And yet, that was precisely what was happening. After leaving Tristan behind to face Henry's scolding alone, Papa had deposited her in her bedchamber, locking the door behind him to, as he'd put it, prevent her from making matters worse.

So much for her plan to seek Tristan out so they could discuss their elopement. Sitting on her bed with her arms crossed, she huffed a breath for the millionth time. This was *her* life, *her* future. She ought to be the one to decide with whom she spent it. And she intended on making that point very clear to both Henry and Papa once she had the chance to speak with them.

She glared at the locked door and muttered a curse. How long had it been? An hour? Possibly two? Frustrated, she reached for the rose quartz at her neck and allowed its cool presence to soothe her. Only Grandmama would understand that this was about more than some passing attraction. This was about her destiny and somehow, some way–

A scraping sound drew her attention. There was a click and then her bedchamber door opened. Henry appeared, looking more worn out than a pair of old stockings. He stared at her with a dull expression that had the unpleasant effect of making her feel completely rotten.

She stood, uncrossed her arms, took a step forward and raised her chin in an effort to look stronger than she felt. "Where is he?"

"Lilli," Henry began, his voice confirming his exhaustion. He swung the door wide and stepped aside, offering her a glimpse of the hallway beyond. "Papa and I would like to talk to you. If you'd please come with me."

"Not before you tell me where Tristan is."

Her comment, a near shout, seemed to reinvigorate her brother. He drew himself up, transforming into a pillar of pure rigidity. "He's gone. Back to wherever the hell he came from."

The harsh remark was like a slap to the face. It took the wind out of Lilli's sails. She stared at her brother as every hope and dream she'd had of spending her life with Tristan began to crumble. "You sent him away?"

"Of course I did."

"Do you at least have an address? Some means by which to find him?"

"My coachman will take him to a coaching inn from which he'll continue his onward journey tomorrow."

He gestured toward the hallway once more. "Just be thankful I did not challenge him to a duel, or he'd have been dead in the morning."

"I hate you," she said, her defenses cracking. Her eyes began to sting but she'd be damned if she'd let Henry watch her cry. So she took a fortifying breath and forced the tears away. Ignoring his wounded expression, she swept past him with as much regality as she could muster.

Neither spoke as they made their way to the parlor. The only sounds Lilli heard came from servants tidying up, which had to mean the ball was over.

Without permitting Henry to open the parlor door for her, Lilli did it herself and entered the room where she sensed a battle was ready to be waged. It was one she had every intention of winning.

She faced her father who stood by the fireplace. He'd been studying the flames but turned toward her, his mouth set in an unforgiving line.

*Right.*

Lilli braced herself. "If you expect me to apologize for my actions or show embarrassment, I fear you'll be disappointed for I intend to do neither. Mr. Henley is a good man. Our liaison was consensual. He didn't do anything I did not invite him to do."

"Good God." Papa scrubbed a palm over his face.

"Furthermore," Lilli continued undaunted, "he is the only man I envision spending the rest of my life with. Henry had no right to send him away and deny me the future I want with the man of my own choosing."

Henry, hovering near her like a dark cloud, sent her a reproving look.

"Are you quite finished?" Papa asked. Without waiting for her response he shifted his gaze to Henry. "Pour me a drink, would you? I daresay this conversation will need a great deal of fortification." Returning his attention to Lilli, he gestured toward the sofa, "Sit."

"I'd rather stand."

"Of course you would." Muttering something about stubborn women and difficult daughters, Papa claimed one of the armchairs, which was highly unusual since he never sat in the presence of a lady. Not even those related to him.

Lilli held herself perfectly still while Henry saw to the drinks. The fact that her insubordination had not caused her father to order her back to her bedchamber yet was nothing short of miraculous. He'd tolerated a great deal from her over the years, she realized, though nothing as grievous as this. And daring to argue with him now, to stand her ground and raise her voice, would have led to dire consequences indeed for most other daughters.

But remaining calm when the man she loved had been forced from her life was impossible. Thankfully, Papa appeared to understand this somehow, but she also knew it was time to rein in her temper, lest she push him too far.

She watched as he sipped his drink, a thoughtful expression creasing his brow. When he finally set his glass aside on the table beside him, he said, "As much as I want to see you happy, I cannot approve of the match you desire. Though not for the reasons you may think."

"What do you mean?" Lilli asked. She was genuinely curious to hear his thoughts.

Papa studied her briefly. "Are you certain you don't want to sit?"

His calm voice undid her urge to fight. She shrugged one shoulder. "All right."

Once seated opposite him on the sofa and with Henry having occupied the spot beside her, Papa said, "A good marriage requires more than physical attraction, Lilli. For a true love match, like the one I've been fortunate enough to share with your mother, common interests are as important as being of the same class. No, don't argue. Please let me explain."

When she gave a small nod, he continued. "You have received a broad education by myself, Henry, your mother, and your governess. You're fluent not only in English but French and German as well. You have a fondness for science not only born from a curiosity I've always tried to encourage but also because you have a sharp mind that allows you to understand the most complex ideas. Furthermore, you enjoy reading Shakespeare."

"Mostly the comedies," Lilli felt compelled to add.

"Nevertheless, understanding the double entendres and what many consider an outdated language requires a certain sort of skill."

"One that can be acquired with practice," Lilli murmured.

"My point is," Papa said with a sigh, "your life

partner needs to be someone with whom you can share such things. And while I mean no insult toward Mr. Henley, I fear a man of his upbringing will disappoint you over time on account of his inability to meet you on the same level."

Lilli blinked. It was mighty difficult not to take offense to such reasoning. She gripped the armrest and took a few steadying breaths in the hope of dispelling the heat that was starting to form at the top of her head.

"I'm sure you are correct," she said once she'd unclenched her teeth. "However, I do not require a copy of myself in a husband. It is enough that he is well read, as Mr. Henley happens to be. In fact, his knowledge of Shakespeare, particularly pertaining to the plays I myself have the least amount of knowledge about, will without doubt astound you. And while it may be true that I have an interest in science, I know little with regard to current affairs or history, subjects Mr. Henley happens to be very well versed in. In other words, he and I are able to add to each other's knowledge, filling the gaps in each other's education.

"However, of greatest importance of all is the fact that he makes me laugh. Never before have I valued another's company as much as I value his. There's more than attraction between us, Papa. There's a level of understanding – a compatibility – that supersedes all else."

A moment of silence ensued as if everyone needed to let that point settle. And then, from someone other than Papa and Henry, came the words, "Well said."

Lilli turned to find her grandmother standing in the doorway. Papa and Henry had spotted her too now and stood. Lilli followed suit. The dowager countess smiled at Lilli as she moved farther into the room.

"Theodora," Papa said, his voice curt. "This matter does not concern you."

"On the contrary, Peter, you'd be surprised by how much it concerns me."

Lilli's eyes widened. She'd never heard her grandmother speak to her father thus, addressing him by his given name rather than by his title. Casting a look at Papa, she saw his surprise before he managed to school his expression.

"For you see," Grandmama continued, "this situation relates to the rose quartz crystal."

"What?" Papa and Henry asked in unison.

Grandmama lowered herself to a vacant armchair. "Have a seat and I'll tell you."

And so she did. For the next half hour, if the clock on the fireplace mantle was anything to go by, Grandmama spoke of her run–in with a gypsy woman decades ago, her serendipitous meeting with her husband immediately after, and the love matches recently made by three of her granddaughters. "Each had unsuccessful Seasons, but as soon as the crystal was in their possession, love found them. And now they are all happily married."

"To fellow peers," Papa exclaimed. "Eva is now the Countess of Somerset, Henrietta's husband will one day inherit a dukedom, while Annie's marriage has made her the Duchess of Rutland. So in their cases there wasn't much cause for concern, regardless of how their matches came about. But aside from this fact, I have to say that I find your story utterly preposterous. If this is the sort of nonsense you're filling my daughter's head with, I may have to limit the time the two of you spend alone with each other."

"Whether you believe in the stone's power or not is irrelevant," Grandmama remarked as though Papa were a bothersome fly she kept having to swat away. "The only thing of importance here is the fact that it clearly brought Lilliana together with Mr. Henley. She is destined to marry him."

"Ridiculous." Papa reached for his glass and took a long sip. "Magic doesn't exist and the fact that you would sit there and try to convince me otherwise is an insult to my intelligence. Not to mention the fact that I cannot for the life of me comprehend your willingness to support Lilliana's desire to marry a nobody – a former employee, no less. She's your granddaughter, for God's sake."

"Yes, she is," Grandmama said, "which is why her happiness matters more to me than a title, a scandal or–"

"Poverty?" Papa pressed. He gave a humorless laugh. "She'll live in a cottage at best. At worst, she'll end up in a hovel, cooking and cleaning while looking after her children. Worrying if they'll be warm for the winter or if they'll go hungry when Mr. Henley fails to provide."

"He would not fail to provide," Lilli said, her voice stronger than she herself felt at the moment. "Mr.

Henley is not only driven but smart enough to acquire whatever position he sets his mind to."

"Is that so?" Papa asked.

"He did acquire a solid position as Henry's valet," she shot back.

This comment led to an awkward silence until Henry said, "It won't be easy for him to acquire a similar job since I sacked him without reference. Besides, he'd have to earn higher wages if he were to afford a decent home."

"Not necessarily," Lilli said while tamping down the urge to throw something at her brother for being so callous. When Papa and Henry gave her questioning looks she took a deep breath and said, "We can use my dowry."

"Absolutely not," Papa blustered.

"You mean to deny me?" she asked, deliberately infusing her tone with outrage.

"You'll not have my blessing to squander your life, Lilliana, and without that there can be no dowry since your only recourse would be to elope. And before you even begin to ponder such an extreme notion, I would suggest you take some time to consider the ramifications such action would have on your family."

"Perhaps this is where I should tell you that I intend to help the young couple," Grandmama said. "Financially, that is. Should they need it."

"Dear God." Papa sank against his seat, a look of complete and utter despair in his eyes. "This is mutiny."

"What is, dear?" asked Mama as she entered the room. Papa and Henry rose to their feet in greeting, albeit with a half–hearted lack of energy. Papa waved at an empty seat and waited for Mama to claim it before resuming his own.

"Your mother has filled Lilliana's head with nonsense," Papa said.

Mama's eyes widened. "That's a rather damning accusation."

"Apparently, Grandmama is of the opinion that Lilli is fated to be together with Mr. Henley due to the powers of a magical stone," Henry said. To his credit, he managed to do so with a straight face, for which Lilli was grateful.

"Oh dear," said Mama. She suddenly frowned. "The same Mr. Henley who works for you?"

"Until I found him in the garden with Lilli earlier," Henry said. "Upon which I promptly sacked him."

"Goodness." Mama glanced at each of them in turn, her expression filled with interest. "It would appear as though this evening has been more eventful than I imag-ined. I can't believe I'm only just learning of all this now. Shame on you, Peter, for not informing me sooner."

Papa set his jaw. "I was hoping to spare you the sordid details."

"I see." Mama reached for Papa's glass of brandy and took a long sip. She then requested a refill from Henry before asking Papa, "How do you intend to deal with the situation?"

"By marrying Lilliana off to a suitable gentleman as soon as possible."

"An excellent plan," said Mama while Lilli tamped

down the urge to scream. Looking like a madwoman would not help counteract Papa's notion of her being slightly cracked in the head for believing a stone could play matchmaker. "Have you any particular prospects in mind?"

"Henry and I have both agreed either Mr. Ershwin or Mr. Newhurst would make an excellent choice."

"Wonderful," Lilli said while directing a glare at her brother. "Mama and I shall also be putting together a list of ladies who'd be delighted to become your viscountess."

"This isn't about me," Henry growled.

"Oh, but it could be," Lilli informed him with exaggerated sweetness. "I'll dub it 'project marrying off Henry.'"

"Don't you–"

"That's quite enough." Grandmama said, the firmness in her tone effectively reining in everyone. Not even Papa looked like he would dare say anything more. The dowager countess took a deep breath and expelled it. "Your intention to marry Lilli off to one of these men is noteworthy. By all means, proceed."

"But I thought," Lilli began, her stomach dropping at the prospect of losing her grandmother's support. Without it, a future with Tristan would be hard, perhaps even impossible, without the resources needed to find out where he had gone.

Grandmama's green eyes caught Lilli's. A smile curved the edge of her lips. "Don't fret. Everything will turn out as it should."

"Exactly," said Papa. "I'll invite both gentlemen back for a visit first thing in the morning."

Lilli shook her head. She felt let down, deserted in her hour of need by the one person she had believed she could count on.

Mama stood. "It's been a long day. Come, Lilliana. I'll escort you to your room."

Lilli moved as though every limb in her body were filled with lead. Drained and defeated in a way she'd never experienced before, she found it impossible to shirk the heaviness in her heart. In a lackluster voice she failed to recognize as her own, she bid her grandmother, Papa, and Henry goodnight and made her way back upstairs.

It wasn't until she entered her bedchamber that she recalled her mother's presence when she ordered Lilli's maid away. The door closed and Lilli dropped onto the bed.

"I know things look bleak at the moment," Mama said as she sat beside her. She took Lilli's hand in her own. "But you must have faith. If you and Mr. Henley are truly meant to be together, nothing will prevent Fate from making that happen."

Stupefied by her mother's words, Lilli turned to meet her gaze. "What are you saying?"

"There's no sense in trying to make Papa understand. He'll never believe in the rose quartz's power. But if *you* do, then ought you not have faith in its ability to make certain you marry the man you are fated to be with?"

Lilli stared at Mama. "You know of the crystal?"

"Of course I do." A soft smile curved Mama's lips. "It brought my parents together and, it would seem, made certain your cousins found love as well."

"But what about you? I mean, it was my understanding none of Grandmama's children made use of its power."

"Well…"

"What?" Lilli prompted.

"I may have snuck it to a ball without telling anyone. The same ball where I just happened to meet your father."

"Really?"

"Yes." Mama's hand squeezed Lilli's. "If Mr. Henley truly is the man you're intended to be with, then you will marry him one way or the other. But you must relinquish control. Otherwise there is no telling whether your union was brought on by your determination to make it happen or because it was destined to be so. Do you understand?"

Lilli nodded. "You want me to step aside and let Papa try and marry me off to someone else. Because the only man I'll actually manage to wed if the stone truly works is the one I'm fated to be with."

"Precisely."

Grandmama's unwillingness to fight Papa on the issue began making sense. Lilli leaned against Mama and gave her a sideways hug. "Thank you."

"I do wonder at the stone's choice however," Mama murmured. "Not to sound like a snob, but as nice as Mr. Henley may be, he doesn't quite seem the right sort for a lady of your breeding."

"Grandmama believes there may be more to him than meets the eye, like being the distant relation to an earl and on the cusp of inheriting both a title and fortune."

"Hmm… That would certainly make for an interesting turn of events."

Mama stood and rang the bell–pull to summon Lilli's maid before saying good night. As soon as she departed, Lilli flopped back onto her bed. It had been a long day and she was verily exhausted. But things no longer appeared as bleak as they had half an hour earlier.

Bolstered by her mother's words, she vowed to be the dutiful daughter her father expected her to be. She'd meet with Mr. Ershwin and Mr. Newhurst when they came to call, confident in the fact that her path would soon cross with Tristan's once more.

# CHAPTER EIGHT

Despite the dire circumstances Tristan had left behind when he'd gone off to seek employment, nothing prepared him for Iris's despair upon his return. She burst into tears as soon as he entered the parlor and found her. And as he hugged her close, her delicate shoulders shook while muffled sobs squeezed at his heart.

"What is it?" He ran a soothing hand over her back and did his best to squash his rising panic. "What's happened?"

"I am…I am…to be…married," she choked out between gulps of air.

The breath seized in Tristan's lungs, trapped there until he managed to hiss it free. His hold on his sister tightened while thoughts poured through his mind. *You're only sixteen. You've not even made your debut. This simply can't be.*

Forcing himself to exude an air of calm for her sake,

he eased away just enough to face her, handed her a handkerchief, and gently asked, "To whom?"

She dabbed at her red–rimmed eyes, then at her nose. "To Baron Shrewsberry."

It took every ounce of control Tristan possessed not to roar at her pronouncement. Allowing his fury free rein wouldn't make Iris feel better. Nor would it help the situation as a whole. But the very idea of Papa agreeing to hand his daughter over to an old lecher like Shrewsberry made Tristan's skin crawl.

Married twice before, the baron had an uncanny ability to outlive wives who were decades younger than he. Whether because he possessed an almost supernatural degree of good health or because the poor women gave up on living once shackled to him, Tristan did not know. What he was absolutely certain of was that he would do all in his power to make sure Iris remained safe from the man.

He found a smile he'd not believed he had in his possession. "Don't worry. I'll speak with Papa."

More like murder him where he stood unless he saw reason.

"And say what?" Iris slumped into a chair with all the appearance of a drooping flower. "This match was Papa's idea. He approached Shrewsberry because he knows the man favors young girls and that he's been struggling to find a new bride whose parents will give their consent."

"Your consent is required as well," Tristan gritted.

"And I shall give it," Iris said. She raised her chin

and straightened her back, showing strength for the first time since Tristan's arrival. "For Emma's sake."

"For…" Tristan blinked. "No. You do not have to sacrifice yourself for any of us. Emma wouldn't want that any more than I do."

"One of us deserves to marry well and with the funds made available to me through marriage, Emma will be able to have a proper debut. Shrewsberry already agreed to cover the expense. It's in the contract."

"The contract is already drawn?" Tristan could scarcely believe it. No one had mentioned a thing. Not one word about any of this in the letters he had received from Mama or from Iris during his absence.

As if reading his thoughts, Iris told him, "We knew you'd protest, so we thought it best not to tell you since it's the only way forward for our family."

"What the hell does that mean?" Tristan asked, the control he'd held on his anger finally slipping.

"It means Papa has gambled away whatever money you sent us."

"How can that be when I sent those funds to Mama so she could make sure they were spent on necessities? Which she assured me they would be when she wrote to thank me."

"You know she hates confrontation as much as I do," Iris told him. "All Papa had to do was show his anger and she relented."

Tristan pushed his fingers through his hair. "Dear God. This is a nightmare."

"The wedding is to take place in a couple of weeks." Iris's voice cracked as fresh tears slid down her cheeks. With a sniff, she swiped them away.

"We'll run away and take Emma with us. Anything to escape this."

"What?" Iris stared at him, wide-eyed.

"Surely you must have thought of such a recourse yourself." He couldn't imagine her not doing so.

"Of course I have, but what sort of life would that be? There's no guarantee a worse fate won't find us. Emma is only ten and since you'd have to work, you'd not be there to protect her or me. What if one of us gets sick? What if you die and leave us penniless?"

"I can assure you I've no intention of dying."

"Of course you don't, but people get sick and accidents happen. I'll not risk putting Emma through something like that. Better I marry so she can have the life she deserves."

Tristan hated Iris's logic, but she was right. By running away they might make things worse, and with a ten year old in tow, it would be a highly irresponsible risk to take. But they couldn't leave Emma behind either. Not with a father who'd stoop as low as he'd done with Iris.

Somehow he'd have to think of another way out. But first, he had a few words to exchange with his father.

"Very well," he told Iris. "But I still mean to tell Papa I'm against this. If you'll excuse me?"

"Of course. Mama is having tea with Mrs. Grisham

and won't be home until later, but you'll probably find Papa in his study."

"Thank you." Tristan bent to kiss his sister's cheek.

"And Tristan," Iris said before he managed to leave the room. When he glanced her way she said, "Please look in on Emma afterward. She'll be in that hideout you built for her in the attic, which is where she's spent most of her time since my betrothal was announced."

The anguish those words brought him could not be measured. He'd been gone, content in the misplaced knowledge that he was helping his sisters. While he'd been caught up in romantic bliss with Lilli, they had both been suffering heartache.

He should have known better. He ought to have realized Papa wouldn't change – that nothing he did to help would make his father a better man.

Furious, Tristan burst into his study. The door flew wide, slamming against the wall. Something rattled and Papa looked up from behind his desk. He stared at Tristan with such apathy Tristan's anger instantly spiked.

"What the hell do you think you're doing?" Tristan demanded. He marched forward, planted his palms on the desk, and glared into Papa's uncaring eyes. "How dare you marry Iris off to a man like Shrewsberry?"

"How dare you burst into my study without a by your leave?" Papa countered, matching Tristan's tone and glare. "Show some respect."

"I'll do so once you've earned it. As of right now, however, my understanding is that you've squandered the funds I sent and made a deal with the devil in order to dig yourself out of the mess you've made."

"If you'd simply found a suitable heiress, we wouldn't be having this discussion," Papa seethed. "Instead, you decided to sully the family name by seeking employment. As if such paltry funds can even begin to cover our cost of living."

Straightening, Tristan told him bluntly, "They would have helped if you'd saved them and spent them wisely rather than gambling them away."

Papa shook his head. "I tried, but then the debt collectors came to call. Again. This time with threats to take the house. I had to quadruple the money for even the slimmest chance of having enough to settle all the bills. The taxes owed to the Crown make up the greatest portion. I saw no other way out. In exchange for Iris's hand in marriage, Shrewsberry will settle my debts after which he'll provide me with a monthly allowance. In addition to this he will pay for Emma's debut and ensure she has a substantial dowry."

"And in exchange he gets Iris."

Papa hesitated briefly before confessing, "He'll be getting this property too."

"What?"

"It's not entailed, Tristan, and considering the expense he'll be covering, I had to agree to his terms."

"In other words, you will in effect become Shrewberry's tenant?" Tristan muttered a curse when what he really wanted to do was punch holes through walls. Or strangle his father. "And you worried I would bring shame to the family by seeking honest work?"

"No one will know."

"Oh really? People will simply believe Iris fell in love with a decrepit pervert and that by some miracle your luck turned?" Tristan stared down his nose at the man who threatened to ruin all of their lives. "Nobody is that blind or stupid, so trust me when I tell you the whole world will know you've sold your daughter to save your own skin."

"What the hell would you have had me do?" Papa shouted, his face turning a deep shade of red.

"Anything but this," Tristan shot back. When Papa didn't respond, Tristan took a moment to let all the details sink in. Shoving his hands in his pockets he crossed to the window and stared at the garden, where too many weeds revealed the lack of the gardener they'd had to sack.

Beyond the old oak tree he could glimpse part of the farmland that had been in his family for generations. The property was vast, consisting of twenty acres he'd one day been meant to inherit. It now appeared he'd be forced to step aside and let Shrewsberry take it.

His fingers curled into fists. Tension hardened his posture.

*No.*

*Not in this lifetime.*

He turned to his father, every hope and dream he'd ever enjoyed aligning themselves until the solution he sought became clear. It wasn't ideal – there was a good chance he'd fail – but with both love and heritage at stake, he had to give it his best shot.

"I want to counter Shrewsberry's offer," he told Papa firmly.

Papa straightened. The look in his eyes was skeptical at best. "What can you possibly do to save our family from ruin?"

"I can marry an earl's daughter." He spoke with the confidence of a man for whom this was a simple matter, as if he would not have to pray neither Henry nor Stratham would shoot him dead upon his return to Stratham House.

Papa's eyes widened and he began to laugh. "You? Marry an earl's daughter? Well, I've never."

"I'll need you to draft a letter," Tristan continued, ignoring his father's outburst, "in which you declare Henley House and all its property mine upon marriage. In exchange, I'll sign a document promising you a monthly allowance, just as Shrewsberry did."

"My God. You're actually serious?"

"Deadly so," Tristan muttered. He crossed his arms and glared at his father. "Well?"

"Impossible. The contract between your sister and the baron has already been drawn. The first banns have been called. The wedding's to take place in only two weeks–"

"Give me one week, Papa. Allow me the chance to save Iris from this fate and for me to marry the woman I love."

Papa blinked. "You fell in love with an earl's daughter? How on earth is that even possible, Tristan?"

"I'll explain all of that later. For now, however, I'd say we have little time to spare." With a three day ride ahead and the clock ticking down toward Iris's wedding, haste was of the essence. "Will you draft the letter or not?"

Papa shook his head. "I made a promise to Shrewsbury. It would be ungentlemanly of me not to keep it."

"You and I both know that a promise made to a scoundrel has no bearing."

"Nevertheless, he has the means to save us while I cannot imagine your plan being more than a dream."

"You're not wrong," Tristan admitted. Papa offered an arrogant snort. Ignoring it, Tristan said, "But you can't deny that if I am able to pull this off, it will have a better outcome for all of us, yourself included."

"I suppose an earl would make a more prestigious relation than a baron," Papa murmured.

Tristan met his gaze. "Does that mean I have your agreement?"

An unbearable moment of silence passed. Papa frowned. He seemed to consider. Tristan held his breath.

"Very well," Papa finally muttered. He opened his desk drawer and retrieved a crisp piece of paper with a slowness that made Tristan feel like a vein might pop in his head at any second. "I'll do what I can to help you achieve the match you desire since it is, as you describe it, in all of our best interests."

Tristan chose not to comment. Instead, he thanked the Lord for Papa's willingness to cooperate, no matter his reason, and began to dictate. Half an hour later, with his father's assurance in hand and his own promise of financial support still freshly signed on the desk, Tristan took his leave.

"Hold on a second," Papa said as Tristan strode to the door. "Does this earl's daughter love you in return?"

Lilli had told him she did, but that was before she'd known he was lying. To his father he said, "I bloody well hope so."

# CHAPTER NINE

Lilli sipped her tea with smug satisfaction. It was almost one week since she'd seen Tristan last, and during that time Papa had done all in his power to encourage Mr. Ershwin's and Mr. Newhurst's interests in her. Sadly, however, Mr. Ershwin had come down with a terrible cold immediately after the masquerade ball and had sent his regrets in response to the luncheon Papa had invited him to. Meanwhile, Mr. Newhurst had shown up, but as soon as he'd stepped from his carriage a wasp had stung him, resulting in an allergic reaction and his prompt departure.

Both gentlemen had vowed to call upon her at a later date. Until then, Papa had scoured the nearby countryside for additional options, resulting in an excursion with Viscount Billsford, who'd stopped by a neighboring township to visit his sister. Unfortunately, he'd tripped over a fallen branch and twisted his ankle while walking with Lilli and her parents through the woods.

"You see?" Grandmama said, her question directed at Papa. "Fate won't allow her to end up with anyone other than the man she is destined to be with."

"Nonsense," said Papa, though the comment held less force than usual. He waved one hand in the air. "You're reading too much into something that's no more than pure coincidence."

"Um hmm." Grandmama gave Lilli a knowing look accompanied by a conspiratorial smile.

"Have you other prospects in mind, dear?" Mama asked Papa.

"Not yet," he grumbled.

"Then I suppose we must wait for one of these men to recover and make an appearance," Mama said.

"It is curious though," Henry said. He'd just finished eating a cucumber sandwich. "What exactly is the likelihood of getting stung by a wasp the moment one steps from a carriage?"

"Not very high, I'll wager," Mama murmured.

"And yet it happened," Papa said while frowning into his teacup. "Which means it's possible."

"But for all three men to suddenly–"

"I realize it's unusual," Papa said, cutting Henry off, "but there's nothing to be done besides hope each one makes a swift recovery."

"Or maybe it's time to call Mr. Henley back?" Grandmama said.

The suggestion was so welcome yet so outrageous, Lilli immediately choked on her tea. Henry came to her aid, slapping her on the back and ordering someone to fetch her a glass of water. Meanwhile Papa had begun to protest, enumerating the many reasons why Mr. Henley would never marry his daughter. Not in a million years.

"In fact," Papa said as a glass of water was thrust into Lilli's hand, "even if he were the last remaining bachelor on earth, I would never, ever, agree to such an atrocious match."

Which was precisely when the butler arrived to announce, "Mr. Henley is here to see you, my lord."

It took great effort for Tristan to keep his nerves under control. Standing in the earl's study anticipating the man's arrival, he clasped his hands behind his back and tried to take steady breaths. When he'd last been here, he'd had nothing to offer a woman of Lilli's station. He'd been her brother's servant for heaven's sake, beneath her in every way.

But this was no longer the case. Now he'd the chance to prove himself worthy, and while he realized he had no title or fortune, he was desperate enough to do his utmost to win her.

The door opened and to Tristan's surprise and relief, Henry arrived instead of his father. He stood in the doorway, staring Tristan down before finally saying, "You've some nerve, showing up here again."

"Agreed," Tristan said.

"Just be glad I convinced Papa to see you in his stead, or I would be figuring out what to do with your corpse right now." He stepped into the room and closed the door while Tristan suppressed a shudder. "Why have you come?"

"To ask for your sister's hand in marriage."

"Are you mad?"

"Not in the least." Tristan faced the viscount's shocked expression with steely resolve. "My hope is to gain your forgiveness first. Truth is, I misled you in an attempt to save my family from destitution. Now, I come to you with an offer – one I hope your father will also be willing to hear."

Henry frowned. "Explain yourself, Tristan."

The use of his given name gave Tristan hope. He took a deep breath. "I am gentry. My father owns a landed estate passed down through three generations. But his fondness for card play, excessive spending, and overall mismanagement of funds have proven calamitous for my family. I saw no other recourse but to seek work in an effort to help pay the debts. Your notice regarding the need for a valet came at the right time. But I knew you'd never consider a gentleman for the position, so I chose not to mention it. Revealing the truth was also too shameful. And when it came to Lilliana, I still had nothing to offer and didn't believe myself worthy."

"What's changed?" Henry asked, his posture stiff and unyielding.

"A number of things. First, I must confess that as much as I love Lilliana, I'm not only here to win her but also to save my eldest sister, Iris, from having to marry Baron Shrewsberry. She's only sixteen and–"

"You need not explain any further. I'm familiar with

the scoundrel." With his features set in stone, Henry crossed to the sideboard. "Brandy?"

Tristan breathed a sigh of relief. "Please."

"I trust your father arranged a match between your sister and Shrewsberry in an attempt to refill his coffers," Henry said while pouring the drinks.

"You are correct." He accepted the glass Henry offered and took a fortifying sip. "Papa made a deal with him, one I'm hoping I might use to my own advantage."

"How so?"

"In the event I marry Lilliana, the deed to Henley House will be transferred to me. My father would receive a monthly allowance, but I would be in charge of managing the estate henceforth. My sister Iris would avoid a terrible fate, I would acquire a wife I love beyond all reason and who, I hope, loves me enough to forgive my deception. But there's no denying the fact that I would need control of her dowry in order to turn things around."

Henry took a deep swallow from his brandy, gave Tristan a thoughtful look and said, "I think it might be best if I ask Papa and Lilliana to join us."

"Are you sure?

Henry chuckled. "You'll have to face them sooner or later if you intend to proceed with this plan. Best sooner I'd say, so you save yourself from having to explain this muddle several times over."

"But do you think your father will even be amenable to the idea after all I've done?"

"If you're referring to your ungentlemanly lack of

restraint with regard to Lilliana, I suggest you avoid the subject and focus on how you intend to acquire his blessing."

With that Henry departed, leaving Tristan no less nervous than he'd been half an hour before.

Elation filled Lilli from head to toe the moment she entered her father's study and saw Tristan. He was truly here. When the butler had announced him, her heart leapt. She'd scarcely dared believe it. So remaining in the parlor while Henry met with him first had not been easy. But one swift look at Papa had informed her she'd best not test him. So she'd sat utterly still, pretending invisibility, until Henry returned to calmly request Papa's and her attendance.

"I've nothing to say to that man," Papa said.

"On the contrary, I think you ought to hear him out," Henry had told him, then added, "I'm glad I did."

"Fine. But Lilliana stays here." Papa stood. "I'll not have her anywhere near him."

"I was of a like mind until a few minutes ago," Henry said, "but I'd like you to trust me, Papa. Lilliana needs to hear what he has to say as well."

Additional arguing had ensued until Papa grudgingly conceded and agreed to let her join them.

Now her gaze met Tristan's, the affectionate look in his eyes warming her until it felt like her whole body sparkled. It lasted but a second before he turned his attention to Papa. "Thank you, my lord, for agreeing to meet."

"Considering my last encounter with you, I've a good mind to run you through." Papa shifted his gaze toward the sword that hung on display above the fireplace.

"Duly noted." Tristan held Papa's gaze as if daring him to make good on his threat. Hard lines around his mouth accentuated the underlying determination with which he'd come.

Lilli's heart beat faster.

"Say what you must then," Papa ordered. "I've no mind to stand about here for the rest of the day."

"My lady," Tristan said, addressing her with a gentleness that stood in stark contrast to his rigid posture. "Perhaps you'd like to sit?"

Since the room contained only three chairs, Lilli declined the offer. "I'm fine. Please proceed."

The edge of Tristan's mouth drew slightly upward, revealing the barest hint of a smile. "Very well. For starters I think it prudent to make one thing perfectly clear. I love you, Lilli. Your ability to look beyond position and station and see a person for who they are at their core has captivated my heart entirely. I love you for your boisterous nature, your energetic approach to life, and your joyful spirit. Your fondness for your family, the concern you show toward the dowager countess, and the affectionate way in which you speak of your parents and brother reflect your caring nature. You've a gentler side I'm sure is often missed on account of your forceful vitality."

He paused for a second, allowing Lilli to return to solid ground. Because the way he described her not only confirmed his love, it proved that he truly saw her. Not simply as the lady she'd been raised to be or the restless girl who'd always struggled with every rule of propriety forced upon her, but as a person with wonderful characteristics.

Even as her eyes misted with deep emotion, she dared a glimpse at Papa and noted his features had softened to some degree.

"As Lord Islington's employee, however," Tristan continued, "I knew you were beyond my reach. It was wrong of me to enjoy your company as I did since nothing could ever come of it. But with each passing moment we shared, adding distance grew harder until…" He cleared his throat and straightened his back. "In a way, I'm thankful to Islington for ending my employment and forcing me away, because it provided me with the only opportunity I'll ever have of trying to win you in earnest. As a gentleman."

"Tristan, you know I'd have–"

"Lilliana," Papa warned with cutting efficiency.

Tristan glanced at him before shifting his gaze back to her. "Whatever hasty idea you may have had, Lilli, I would never have let you implement it."

Silence followed as everyone absorbed that statement. Blood rushed through Lilli's veins. She could scarcely believe it. The man she loved and who'd just declared loving her in return would not have agreed to elope with her after the masquerade if they had not been discovered?

As if hearing her unspoken question he said, "The last thing I'd ever want is to wreck your life and leave you worse off than before you met me. With nothing to offer, I saw no point in telling you the truth since I didn't believe it would make any difference. Until I returned home and learned of a deal my father made with Baron Shrewsberry."

"Shrewsberry?" Papa practically spat the name. "What the hell does he have to do with all this?"

"He's engaged to my sister, Iris, who's only sixteen years of age," Tristan said, the disgust he felt at the very idea evident in his twisted expression.

Lilli took a sharp breath. Grandmama had been right. The stone would not make an impossible match which had to mean…

"You're more than what you gave yourself out to be," she said with rising excitement. "You must be if a baron is willing to marry into your family."

"I'm gentry," Tristan admitted. "Though I dare say the tenant farmers working my family's land are better off financially than I am."

"Of course." Lilli struggled to contain her laughter. "It all makes perfect sense now."

"It does?" asked Tristan, Henry, and Papa in unison.

"Naturally." She cleared her throat and began to explain. "Tristan, Mr. Henley, that is was likely forced to seek work in order to make ends meet at home. But since Henry wouldn't have hired a gentleman to be his servant and taking on such a position would have brought shame to his family, Mr. Henley chose not to mention the fact."

"So you're not angry with me for concealing my heritage?" Tristan carefully asked with a hint of skepticism.

"Only in the sense that it has delayed a positive outcome for us but otherwise no. I understand your reasoning and the duty compelling you to protect your family's reputation. And the truth is, it doesn't change who you really are or the fact that you love me. Does it?"

"Not in the least." A slight crack in his voice revealed his emotion.

"Don't ever deceive me again though," Lilli told him firmly. "Or the next time you go for a walk you'll likely find yourself knee deep in one of *my* holes."

Tristan's features relaxed into a grin that felt like summer in the middle of winter.

"I'm not sure what the two of you are going on about now," Papa said, his crisp voice ruining the levity of the moment, "but I would like to know how Mr. Henley, who's just declared himself a penniless liar, hopes to acquire my blessing."

Bolstered by Lilli's support – her undeniable faith in him – Tristan began to explain. He left nothing out as he detailed his father's poor handling of the family finances and the deal Tristan had struck with him. When he finished he said, "It is imperative you believe me when I say that the need I have for your daughter's dowry has no bearing on how I feel about her. I love her to distraction, my lord."

"On that score I have no doubt," Stratham said while studying Tristan in a manner that made him feel like squirming. "It shows in every aspect of your being. What concerns me is the lack of evidence I have regarding your ability to run an estate and grow the investments you mean to make. You've no experience in that regard."

"Correct," Tristan said. The hope he'd harbored a short while ago began to slip from his grasp. "Failure isn't an option, however. Not when my family's future depends upon my success."

The earl was silent a moment. Tristan's heart raced.

"You were pleased with Mr. Henley's performance while he was in your employ, were you not?" Stratham eventually asked his son while studying Tristan thoughtfully.

"Very much so," Henry said.

"He was hard working, dependable, and thorough?"

"Without fail."

"Here is my proposal then," Stratham said, his businesslike manner sending a new jolt of confidence through Tristan's veins. "I shall be assessing and advising you over the course of the next year. You'll make no decisions involving Lilliana's dowry without my approval. Furthermore, she shall always have an equal say in how the funds are spent. I'll want all of this in writing."

"Agreed," Tristan said, his pulse leaping with the

knowledge that Stratham was already in the process of outlining the marriage contract.

"Once the year is up," Stratham continued, "I'll review your abilities. If you live up to my expectations, I'll step aside and let the two of you manage things on your own. But if you don't, I'll continue keeping watch until the next year is up, and so on."

"So then," Lilli began, her gaze darting back and forth between Tristan and her father. "Does that mean—"

"Yes, yes. You can have him if that's what you truly—"

Her squeal drowned out the remainder of Stratham's words as she flung herself into Tristan's arms and kissed him, right there in the middle of her father's study. It was unthinkable, the lack of propriety absolutely unquestionable, yet so very perfect and necessary.

Her lips were warm and soft, inviting and a treat best saved for later when they were alone. He eased her away and told her father, "I'll have to return home immediately if I'm to stop my sister from marrying Shrewsberry."

"Henry and I will escort you," Stratham announced. "Our presence ought to encourage your father to follow through on his promise."

"Agreed," Henry said. "But before we depart we probably ought to celebrate Tristan's betrothal to Lilli in style. If I may, I'd like to suggest a champagne toast in the parlor or it's unlikely Mama and Grandmama will ever forgive us."

"You're right," Stratham said. "A quick drink and then we'll be off."

He led the way from the study with Henry immediately behind him while Tristan and Lilli took up the rear. Tristan caught Lilli's hand and gave it a squeeze. "Happy?"

"Unquestionably so," she whispered and drew him into an alcove for a much more smoldering kiss than the one they'd enjoyed in the study. It fairly lit Tristan's soul on fire and made him forget time and place for a second. Sweeping his arm around her, he held her while letting her passion consume him.

"Where the devil are they?" Stratham inquired, his voice prompting a laugh from Tristan and Lilli alike.

"Come. I think we'd best join the rest of the party," Tristan said with no small amount of regret. Taking her by the hand, he led her to the parlor where congratulations awaited.

He watched with happiness in his heart as she embraced her mother and the dowager countess. Somehow, against all odds, he'd won the woman he loved. And he would do all in his power to honor, protect, and support her. Until his dying breath.

# EPILOGUE

"We really ought to get up," Lilli told Tristan while doing very little to follow through on her words. Instead, she snuggled further into her husband's embrace.

A deep chuckle vibrated through him, prompting her lips to curve in a smile that was pressed against his chest as she kissed him. His hold on her tightened, bringing her closer. "Our guests aren't due for another hour at least."

"Which is roughly how long it will take me to dress and prepare." It had already been two o'clock by the time they'd finished luncheon and headed upstairs for their afternoon 'nap'.

"Not if I serve as your lady's maid," Tristan said. His palm roamed over her bottom with lazy strokes that threatened to drive her mad. He suddenly shifted, rolling her onto her back. Gorgeous dark eyes gazed into hers. "And since we know I'm most efficient, there ought to be time for a few more kisses first."

Resisting him was impossible, so Lilli just sighed with pleasure and gave herself up to another incredible round of lovemaking. It was almost a year since they'd met and during that time the love they shared for each other had deepened.

When she finally managed to climb out of bed after watching Tristan dress, she marveled that her legs could hold her upright. A shift slid over her head and her arms were gently pulled through the sleeves. Stays followed along with a pair of silk stockings with tiny red roses embroidered along each side. Lastly, Tristan helped her put on her gown.

Standing behind her, he planted a series of kisses along her shoulder as he finished doing up the buttons at her back. "There. No one will know you were being ravished ten minutes ago."

His fingers traced the length of her neck, eliciting a tiny shiver. Heat flooded her cheeks. "You're incorrigible."

"Would you want me any other way?"

Their gazes collided in the mirror. "Never."

Heat filled his eyes. One of his hands settled firmly against her waist. He moved in closer and pressed his lips to the edge of her jaw.

"Tristan." She'd meant to reprimand him. Instead the breathiness with which she spoke revealed her desire. The devilish scoundrel had managed to stoke it again with the slightest of ease.

His hand slid lower.

Lilli leaned into his solid embrace, allowed herself to be seduced by that wondrous scent so innately his: a touch of sandalwood mixed with bergamot, musk, and a hint of ocean breeze.

A knock sounded. "Mr. and Mrs. Henley?"

Tristan muttered a curse. "Yes?"

"Your guests have arrived," the butler informed them, his voice slightly muffled by the door.

"Please show them to the parlor," Lilli told him. "We'll be down in a moment."

Tristan sighed, pressed one last kiss to Lilli's shoulder, and stepped away. "I suppose we'd better put in an appearance."

Lilli smiled broadly as she turned to accept the arm he offered.

She'd never been prouder of anyone in her life. Since their wedding, Tristan had proven himself not only a capable landowner and a successful investor, but also a thoughtful husband who valued his wife's opinion. He'd been firm but kind with regard to his father, and while Lilli knew her own Papa must have tested Tristan's patience on occasion, he'd never complained. Instead, he'd listened and learned, implementing every piece of advice he received until every debt had been paid and the property could be credited with a significant income.

"There you are," said Grandmama the instant Lilli and Tristan entered the parlor. She sent them a wry smile. "We were wondering what might be keeping you."

"Don't mind her," Lilli's cousin, Eva, said while rocking Robert, her one-year-old son, in her arms.

"We're all thrilled to be here. It's high time you hosted a house party."

"We wanted to wait until the weather improved," Tristan explained.

Glancing around, Lilli welcomed all the familiar faces. Annie sat beside Lilli's mother on the sofa, her position slightly awkward on account of her large belly. Her husband, the Duke of Rutland, stood behind her, one hand resting lightly upon her shoulder.

Meanwhile, Henrietta watched her husband with deep adoration while he cradled their sleeping daughter, Jane, in his arms.

"I hope you won't think it too forward, but I took the liberty of ordering tea for us all," Papa said.

"I'm glad you did," Lilli said as she went to embrace him. "We want all of you to feel right at home."

Additional hugs followed as greetings were exchanged. Tristan's father joined the party a few minutes later as well. He brought both Iris and Emma with him.

"I understand Lilliana will be helping you with your debut this Season," Grandmama said, her comment directed at Iris, who now sat at Lilli's left.

"Yes," Iris said. "She has been most kind, though I must confess, it's all a bit overwhelming."

"It was for us too," Annie said. She glanced at her husband as if he'd invented the stars. "But we found our happily ever afters, and so shall you."

"I'm not so sure." Iris spoke so low Lilli doubted anyone else had heard her.

Lilli leaned in. "Don't worry. When the time is right, I'll lend you the rose quartz crystal."

Iris frowned. "I don't understand. How is that going to help with anything?"

"You'll see," Lilli promised. The stone had worked wonders for Grandmama, for Mama too it would seem, for Eva, Annie, Henrietta, and for herself. She smiled, content in the knowledge that it would do so for Iris as well.

On this thought Lilli glanced at Tristan who appeared to be in deep conversation with her brother. Nevertheless, his gaze shifted, meeting hers from across the room and igniting that same electrical spark she'd experienced when they'd first met.

Love had grown between them from that moment onward, more beautifully than any words Shakespeare had ever written. And it was all thanks to the extraordinary power of a mystical gem.

~

Ready for another story? Check out *Mr. Donahue's Total Surrender!*

And sign up for my newsletter at www.sophiebarnes.com so you don't miss out on my freebies, special deals, and giveaways. You'll receive a complimentary copy of *No Ordinary Duke* with your subscription!

Did you enjoy *Only the Valet Will Do*? If so, please take a moment to leave a review since this can help other readers discover books they'll love.

**Keep turning for my author's note and for a sneak peek of *Mr. Donahue's Total Surrender!***

Get a sneak peek from another romance you'll love!
Keep reading for an excerpt from
Mr. Donahue's Total Surrender
*An Enterprising Scoundrels novella*

# CHAPTER ONE

*London, 1849*

Calista Faulkner clasped her hands together to keep from fidgeting. Her heart was in her throat. Goodness. She needed this position. Desperately.

Her stomach clenched at that thought. An employer might think her agitation signaled a lack of inexperience. And they'd be right.

She took a deep breath. Forced herself to sit still. After all, she'd not worked a single day in her life. But she was willing to learn, even though she feared she wouldn't be given the chance. Not after being turned away from eight businesses already, as well as an upper class home in need of a governess.

Seated across from her now in this neatly furnished office was yet another man with the power to determine her fate. He'd introduced himself as Mr. Greene, the Hotel Imperial's manager. She'd told him she was Jane Smith for the sake of preserving her anonymity.

It wouldn't do for her real name to get out.

Slim of build with thinning brown hair slicked back, a slender nose, flat mouth, and beady eyes framed by wire-rimmed spectacles, Mr. Greene looked to be in his mid to late fifties.

"Frankly," he said, glancing at the pocket watch he'd placed on his desk, "I don't know what you mean to accomplish here without a letter of reference."

"I was hoping I might be permitted to prove myself capable," Calista said. She added a smile even though he proceeded to scowl. "My accounting skills are impeccable and—"

He stopped her with a snort. "Perhaps if you were to lower your expectations, you'd have more success in gaining employment."

"Right." Calista stared across at him with determination. "I also know what's required of a good maid and"—she swallowed when his eyebrows rose toward his hairline—"I can assure you I shall work hard to live up to the standards this hotel is known for."

"Hmm… You strike me as rather well-spoken. Educated even." Mr. Greene tilted his head while he studied her. She tried to sit perfectly still. "And your accent… American, is it?"

She nodded. "I'm from New York."

"Ah. Well thank you for coming in, Miss Smith. I wish you the best of luck in your…ahem…future endeavors."

Calista blinked. "So you're not hiring me?"

"No."

"Because I don't have references or because I'm American?"

Mr. Greene glanced at the door as if he hoped she'd decide to use it. "To be honest, it's both, but if it makes you feel any better I'd made up my mind before I learned where you're from."

Calista frowned. "Before I even spoke?"

A red hue colored Mr. Greene's cheeks. "While your proposal to work as maid is not entirely ridiculous, I fear you're too pretty. Wives won't trust you to clean their rooms. In case the husband sees you, that is. Again, I'm sorry."

Appalled by his implication that she might tempt a married man to stray, Calista stood, hands fisted at her sides. "Mr. Greene. All I want is honest work and while I may not have experience, I know how to make a bed and how to sweep a floor. Indeed, I'm even able to light a fire if that's what's required of me. These tasks are simple to do. They don't require much skill. As for my looks, they cannot be helped though I must say I disagree with your assessment. I'm not the sort of woman any wife need fear, and the fact that you would suggest as much is offensive to me. That aside, I swear to you that if you give me a chance, you won't be sorry." She took a deep breath and sank back onto her seat. Determined to make one final attempt, she leaned forward and said in earnest, "Please. I need this position."

"While I appreciate your fortitude, you simply aren't suited to work here, Miss Smith. Now please, if you don't mind, this interview is—"

The door opened behind Calista and someone else entered the room.

"A word please, Mr. Greene," a man's voice spoke from behind her.

Mr. Greene scrambled from his chair and crossed the floor. Calista twisted in her seat in an effort to catch a glimpse of the man who'd commanded, rather than asked, Mr. Greene to join him. He was gone from view before she had the chance.

Mr. Greene vanished as well. The door closed and a muted conversation ensued from the opposite side. What on earth was going on? It sounded like there might be some sort of emergency.

She was still trying to work her way through the various reasons for the stranger's interruption when Mr. Greene returned.

He stood for a moment in the doorway, watching her as though she were a riddle he didn't know how to solve.

"Well, Miss Smith," he finally said, "it seems you have a job."

Her jaw dropped. Had he not just dismissed her? She stared at Mr. Greene. Who was this man who'd spoken to him and what had he said to change his mind?

"If you still desire to work here you'll start as a scullery maid in the kitchen."

A scullery maid?

"But—"

"Take it or leave it, Miss Smith." When she didn't respond right away he said, "The pay isn't bad. You'll get ten pounds per annum, which is more than the position is worth, if you ask me."

Calista sank against her chair. At this rate, it would take forever before she'd have enough money to purchase a ticket back to New York.

"What about room and board?" she asked, hoping to

avoid the cost of lodging so she could save more of her salary.

"There's nothing left in the servants' quarters, but I'm sure we can set up a cot for you in the pantry. As long as you're willing to clear it away each morning before you start."

Calista swallowed. This wasn't what she wanted for herself, but she couldn't afford to turn down the offer either. Not when she was running dangerously low on funds. Already, she'd been forced to sell most of the fine dresses she'd brought with her to England. If she refused the position, she'd likely end up on the street. Acquiring a job had proven hard enough without letting pride get in her way.

"Thank you, Mr. Greene." She would be polite and respectful, just as her mother had taught her. Calista stood, reticule in hand. "I'll just collect my things from the boarding house. It's not far, so I shan't be long."

Mr. Greene looked down his nose at her. "When you return, make sure you use the back entrance. The one on the side is reserved for the upstairs staff."

Calista forced a smile. "Duly noted."

When Mr. Greene stared back at her with both eyebrows raised, she bobbed a quick curtsey and took her leave.

One hour later, Calista Faulkner was handed a tub filled with dirty dishes and told to scrub them clean.

Refusing to be disheartened, she forced herself to think of her plan to go home. Surely she could wash dishes. How hard could it be? "Where should I fetch the water from?"

The servant who'd been tasked with getting Calista started, a plump woman Mr. Greene had referred to as Tilda, gave her an incredulous look and pointed toward the stoves. "There are the kettles. Soap's in the pail behind you."

Calista wanted to ask about a sponge or a brush, but Tilda was already walking away. Setting the tub on a nearby work bench, she wrinkled her nose and wondered how best to proceed.

"Well don't just stand there, girl," the cook snapped. "Get on with it or get out. We've not the time to rest on our laurels 'round 'ere."

"What do you expect from a fancy foreigner, Mrs. Elkins?" a middle-aged man dressed in a dark suit inquired as he collected the plates that had just been prepared by a maid Calista took to be Mrs. Elkins's assistant. "I wager she'll be sacked before the end of the week."

Considering it was already Thursday, the comment did not bode well. Determined to prove herself capable and earn these people's respect, Calista dumped a measure of soap into the tub, then crossed to the stove and grabbed the kettle. Only to withdraw her hand with an agonized squeal as soon as she touched the hot metal.

Laughter erupted behind her.

"You don't belong in a kitchen," Mrs. Elkins said while Calista's hand began to sting from the burn. "The sooner you realize that, the better."

Calista cursed herself for her foolishness. In her

haste to disprove these people's assumption about her, she'd only lent credence to their opinions.

Furious with herself, she snatched a navy blue potholder from a hook on the wall and grabbed the kettle once more. As soon as the tub was filled with steaming hot water and frothy bubbles, she pondered her next move. A space would have to be prepared for the clean dishes to dry on. She'd figure that out while she waited for the water to reach a more comfortable temperature for her hands.

Eventually, with a dishrag laid out, she considered the fine white porcelain dishes stacked on the table, smeared in leftover gravy and bits of food. Right. Best get on with it then.

Pushing her sleeves up, she grabbed the sponge she'd located under the counter, and proceeded to wash each plate with care.

"I need more plates," someone shouted from the other end of the room.

"Check with the new girl," Mrs. Elkins replied.

Calista froze. She'd only just started washing up a short while ago. She began scrubbing faster just as another tub filled with dirty dishes landed beside her with a clatter.

"Cor," a young man mumbled. "Is that all you've done this past hour? Sammy, come lend a hand here, will you? We need those plates now and this scullery maid is taking forever."

"Let's have a look then," a young girl said as she shouldered Calista out of the way. She surveyed the scene and turned to Calista with sharp disbelief. "You've not even finished rinsing them yet."

"Wha…" Calista stared at the tub filled with water and soap. "I'm washing them."

The girl clucked her tongue. "You mean to tell me you were planning to dry those off and let all the upstairs gents and ladies dine off of them after only one dip? Are you cracked in the head?"

Calista stared back at her, horrified by the pricking sensation now burning behind her eyes. She'd always believed herself to be well educated and smart, and yet she could not do a simple task like washing dishes properly. "I'm sorry. I thought—"

"Well you thought wrong and now there'll be a delay. Heaven above, if Mr. Greene won't have all our hides for this. Move over."

Calista stepped back and watched Sammy rinse off the rest of the dirty plates with swift efficiency. She piled them on the side of the work table, then filled an empty tub with fresh hot water and soap.

"Is there anything I can do to help?" Calista asked while doing her best to ignore the angry stares the rest of the servants were sending her way.

"You can toss the dirty water outside," Sammy said without looking at her. "If you're capable, that is."

Forcing back the tears, Calista picked up the tub and made her way to the door leading out to a court-yard beyond. She would not cry in front of these people. She refused to. And yet, the painful knot in her throat suggested she might do precisely that at any moment, so she rushed through the doorway, sloshing water all over the front of her gown in her haste to disappear from the kitchen and from the censure she had to face there.

Hopefully with time, her situation here would improve, she told herself as she rinsed out the tub at the pump. It was important to be positive and to remember all she accomplished by being here. At least she had a roof over her head and the means by which to earn the money she so desperately needed.

But as the weeks wore on, she realized the hostility she faced would not diminish with time. And while she now knew her way around the kitchen and had learned how to accomplish her chores in a satisfactory manner, she invariably felt as though she risked getting sacked at any moment. It was as though an axe hung over her head, ready to drop on account of the slightest mistake.

It hadn't yet, though Mr. Greene had certainly threatened her with that eventuality more than once. The last time being when a plate she'd been meaning to wash had fallen to the floor and shattered. It hadn't been her fault. She was certain of this. Rather, the blame belonged to a waiter named Richard, who'd been harassing her since her arrival. He'd walked past her spot and pushed the plate straight off the work table.

"Mr. Greene won't be pleased with that," Richard said with a sneer. The young waiter had been particularly cold toward her after she'd threatened him with a knife during her first night in the pantry. His advances had not been welcome. So he did what he could to take revenge.

"I ought to turn you out over this," Mr. Greene said

when he learned what had happened. "Instead, I'll deny you the next month's wages."

Tucked away in the pantry later that night and with the door barricaded against unwanted visitors, Calista swore she would start seeking other employment. The only problem was her breaks were limited. But when she finally did manage to get to an agency, the response she received was no different from the one she'd been given before. References were required and since her only work experience was as a scullery maid, she had no hope of advancing to lady's maid or governess. In fact, advancing to the next position as tweeny would take at least another year of experience, she learned.

Disheartened and unhappy, Calista returned to the Imperial. This was only temporary, she reminded herself and as such, she would simply have to make the most of her dismal situation. She sighed as she crept into bed that night. At this point she would gladly give up the cabin she'd hoped to purchase for her return to New York and settle for the cheapest passage available. It would in all likelihood mean she'd be traveling with the cargo and all the other poor souls who couldn't afford any better. But Calista no longer cared. All she knew was that she had to get away from the Imperial as fast as she possibly could.

ORDER YOUR COPY TODAY!

# AUTHOR'S NOTE

Dear Reader,

Only the Valet Will Do was initially published as part of a box set that included three other stories, all loosely tied together around the magical matchmaking properties of a rose quartz crystal. Each story can be read as a standalone with *Only the Valet Will Do* as the final book in the series. If you would like to read the other books, their titles are as follows:

- Forever My Rogue by Amanda Mariel
- Courting a Christmas Wallflower by Dawn Brower
- Wicked With You by Stacy Reid

As always, thank you for reading my stories. I hope you enjoyed *Only the Valet Will Do* and look forward to sharing more adventures with you in the future.

Sophie

xoxo

# ACKNOWLEDGMENTS

I would like to thank the Killion Group for their incredible help with the editing and cover design for this book.

And to my friends and family, thank you for your constant support and for believing in me. I would be lost without you!

# ABOUT THE AUTHOR

USA TODAY bestselling author, Sophie Barnes, has spent her youth traveling with her parents to wonderful places around the world. She's lived in five different countries, on three different continents, has studied design in Paris and New York, and speaks Danish, English, French, Spanish, and Romanian with varying degrees of fluency. But most impressive of all – she's been married to the same man three times, in three different countries and in three different dresses.

While living in Africa, Sophie turned to her lifelong passion – writing.

When she's not busy dreaming up her next romance novel, Sophie enjoys spending time with her family, cooking, gardening, watching romantic comedies and, of course, reading. She currently lives on the East Coast.

You can contact her through her website at www.-sophiebarnes.com

And please consider leaving a review for this book.

Every review is greatly appreciated!

9 798215 535080